HAUNTED
CEMETERIES

Edrick Thay

GHOST
HOUSE

Ghost House Books

© 2004 by Ghost House Books
First printed in 2004 10 9 8 7 6 5 4 3 2 1
Printed in Canada

The Publisher: Ghost House Books
Distributed by Lone Pine Publishing

10145 – 81 Avenue	1808 – B Street NW, Suite 140
Edmonton, AB T6E 1W9	Auburn, WA 98001
Canada	USA

Website: http://www.ghostbooks.net

National Library of Canada Cataloguing in Publication Data

Thay, Edrick, 1977-
    Haunted cemeteries / Edrick Thay.

ISBN 1-894877-60-8

    1. Haunted cemeteries. I. Title.

BF1474.3.T48 2004	133.1'22	C2004-900151-5

Editorial Director: Nancy Foulds
Project Editor and Illustrations Coordinator: Carol Woo
Production Coordinator: Gene Longson
Cover Design: Gerry Dotto
Layout and Production: Lynett McKell

Photo Credits: Every effort has been made to accurately credit photographers. Any errors or omissions should be directed to the publisher for changes in future editions. The photographs and illustrations in this book are reproduced with the kind permission of the following sources: Niagara Falls Public Library (p. 29: 12690; p. 33: 12677); Matthew James Didier (p. 39); Istock (p. 64: Mary Lane; p. 69, 71: Hayley Easton; p. 73: Daniel Kolman); Library of Congress (p. 67: USZ62-128736; p. 85: USZ62-83665; p. 169: D4-18876); Carol Woo (p. 82, 91, 95, 101); Corbis (p. 115); Douglas W. Welty (p. 153, 157); David Gustafson (p. 183, 185, 189).

The stories, folklore and legends in this book are based on the author's collection of sources including individuals whose experiences have led them to believe they have encountered phenomena of some kind or another. They are meant to entertain, and neither the publisher nor the author claims these stories represent fact.

We acknowledge the financial support of the Government of Canada through the Book Publishing Industry Development Program (BPIDP) for our publishing activities.

PC: P5

To the ghost boys

Contents

Acknowledgments

There are many people to thank for helping make this book possible. Without their assistance and generosity, this volume would be less than what it is.

I owe much gratitude to the dedicated individuals who spend their lives investigating and recording ghostly events. Among them are Chad Patterson of California Society for Ghost Research, Matthew James Didier of the Ontario Ghosts and Hauntings Research Society, Pete Sexton of the Western New York Ghosts and Hauntings Society, Troy Taylor and Brian Roesch, as well as paranormal societies like Eeeek!, Shadowseekers and the Ghost Research Society. Their work helped to bring a sharper focus and immediacy to these accounts and, I hope, a better understanding of the paranormal world.

For her patience and highly entertaining and candid interviews, psychic Barbara Garcia deserves a world of thanks for helping to flesh out the Pink Lady of Yorba Cemetery as well as psychic phenomena.

Kaitlyn of Hamilton, Ontario, who lives next to Burkholder Cemetery, also has my deepest gratitude for allowing me to share her experiences. So too do the many others who submitted accounts to me but chose to withhold their names. I hope you know who you are and that I appreciate all you've done for me. This book would not have been possible without your contributions.

I would also like to thank everyone in the Ghost House family: Shane Kennedy, Nancy Foulds and Chris Wangler helped with the organization and development of this project; without them, there would be nothing but blank pages following this one. Carol Woo once again has managed to find the photos that illuminate my words; she also trimmed the excess verbiage to create a slimmer, sleeker and better text. Lynett McKell has managed to transform a simple document into an honest to goodness book. Thanks and wow.

Finally, many thanks to Lee Craig, Shelagh Kubish, Allan Mott and Dan Asfar, whose contributions to this book were indirect yet invaluable nonetheless. Without their shoulders to lean on, I fear I would have stumbled and stumbled badly. They helped me push through those days when inspiration was scant and scarce; their laughter and their company chased away the clouds and brought a smile to my face. Thank you all very much. You have my eternal gratitude.

Introduction

In late 2001, a class action suit was filed against Menorah Gardens in Fort Lauderdale, Florida, for the desecration and destruction of gravesites. In an attempt to make room for additional graves, the caretakers had allegedly exhumed bodies and tossed them aside as if they were little more than refuse. Other claims made against the company involved the burying of dead in plots other than the ones they had purchased, the crushing of vaults and coffins that contained bodies and the mixing of different bodies within single graves. The story broke over the public like a tidal wave, leaving people horrified and appalled. The national outrage in the wake of the suit speaks to the reverence with which we view cemeteries. Even as cremation becomes more and more common, they continue to occupy a prominent, even sacred, place in our lives.

None of us are long for this world; it's the cemetery that allows us to transcend, however meekly, that fate. The cemetery, after all, is a place of remembrance. The thousands of visitors who journey each year to Cimetière du Père Lachaise in Paris, France, to visit the graves of writer Oscar Wilde or singer Jim Morrison know that much to be true. Though our bodies may become fodder for worms, memory preserves our spirits.

It's an idea best articulated in the beliefs of the ancient Egyptians. Though even the most magnificent modern gravesites are plain and drab when compared to the grand and awesome pyramids, the reasoning behind the creation of both remains the same. To the ancient Egyptians, death was never complete as long as the names of the dead were remembered. To speak the names of the pharaohs was to resurrect their souls. Indeed, who hasn't paused in a cemetery to read names etched upon tombstones without wondering who those individuals may have been in life? It's a simple act borne out of mere curiosity, but in those fleeting moments, the dead are resurrected.

Cemeteries are commonly believed to be among the most haunted places on earth; it's only natural, of course. Since ghosts are, by definition, the disembodied spirits and souls of the dead, if they do exist, then surely they must exist in cemeteries. However, it seems as if cemeteries are as attractive to the spirits as they are to the living. Most cemeteries are decidedly free of the paranormal, as ghosts tend to haunt those places that hold greater personal significance and symbolism—the house they lived in or a street they might have frequented, for example. Of course, there are exceptions.

Greenwood Cemetery in Decatur, Illinois, may be one of the most haunted sites not just in the Midwest, but in the United States. Home to the Greenwood Bride, the Greenwood Lights, the Weeping Woman and a few unfortunate Confederate soldiers, Greenwood Cemetery boasts a wide assortment of spooks and ghosts that have captured the imagination for years. There is also Hollywood Forever Cemetery with its collection of the famous and infamous. Ghosts there range from a woman who continues to mourn at the tomb of screen idol Rudolph Valentino to Virginia Rappe, allegedly killed at the hands of comedian Roscoe "Fatty" Arbuckle.

While some cemeteries are free of ghosts, they may not be entirely free of curses. The ancient Egyptians believed that their dead needed to be provided in the afterlife, and buried their dead in huge tombs packed with treasures and valuables. They knew all too well, as caretakers know today, that these gravesites would be easy marks for tomb raiders and vandals. To deter these thieves, the ancient Egyptians allegedly cursed their gravesites, the most famous of these being the Curse of King Tut, whose tomb was discovered by Howard Carter in 1922.

Though questionable, the idea of a lethal curse, forever associated with the opening of Tutankhamun's tomb, has proven remarkably resilient and continually fascinating. It's this magnetic combination that compels people to visit Howard Street Cemetery and Bucksport Cemetery. The former is where Salem witch trial victim, Giles Corey, still roams, his appearances an omen for some great tragedy, while the latter is home to the gravesite of Bucksport, Maine, founder Jonathan Buck, which a witch may have cursed forever.

Every cemetery has countless stories to tell. Lifetimes, not just bodies, are buried beneath the ground, and lurking within each ghost story is a very real human face. Perhaps that's why ghost stories resonate with the public: even if people don't believe in them, they still prove irresistible and provocative.

Although the term "cemetery" did not come into general English usage until the 15th century, archaeological evidence points to the burying of our dead as a practice that has spanned millennia. In this way, we are still very much connected to even our most primitive of ancestors, who interred their dead in caves, grave mounds and barrows. We share with them the same questions, confusion, anger and sense of loss; despite the wonders of this technological age, despite all the centuries of our evolutions, death still leaves us as raw and exposed as it did our forebears.

The stories in this book come from all over North America and even from as far away as Africa. I've tried to cover investigations of the sites, to illuminate the often misunderstood world of the ghost researcher (or investigator or hunter). I spoke with psychics, most notably Barbara Garcia, in an attempt to understand their particular and mysterious gifts. Many people were willing to share with me their own private encounters with ghosts and I've incorporated many of them into this book, although some names, places and events have been altered to protect people's identities. While these tales of sad, angry, tortured, victimized, saintly and benevolent individuals may not drive you to visit a cemetery after dark anytime soon, I hope that they do cast cemeteries in a slightly different light.

I hope your experience reading these will be similar to those of Kaitlyn in Hamilton, Ontario, who has spent all her life living next to a cemetery. Though she originally found life next to a cemetery somewhat disturbing, her paranormal experiences have given her a different and far more accommodating perspective on cemeteries, death and the afterlife.

El Campo Santo Cemetery

SAN DIEGO, CALIFORNIA

As one of the oldest cemeteries in southern California, El Campo Santo Cemetery has acquired more than its share of eerie and paranormal stories. It is a popular attraction for tourists and San Diegans passing through the Old Town district of this surfing haven along the picturesque Pacific coast. Buried within the small but tidy El Campo Santo Cemetery are members of some of early San Diego's most distinguished families, as well as those who came to California seeking their fortunes only to find that life in the Wild West was cheap and precarious. Men such as Antonio Garra, Thomas Marshall and Santiago "Yankee Jim" Robinson did not have the wealth of people such as Jose Antonio Aguirre, Maria Victoria Dominguez Estudilla and Cave Johnson Couts to insulate them from lawlessness. They may have led very different lives, but in death they have all found some sort of peace in El Campo Santo Cemetery.

Its name, Spanish for "the holy field," pays tribute to the early Spanish explorers who first came to the California coast in the mid-16th century. Spaniards returned again in the early 17th century, when Sebastian Vizcaino made landing in a bay on the feast day of San Diego de Alcala. He named the bay, appropriately enough, San Diego. But Spanish settlement of the area did not begin in earnest until the middle of the 18th century, when the first California mission, San Diego de Alcala, was dedicated in 1769.

In 1849, Juan Adams became the first person to be buried in El Campo Santo Cemetery. Over time, 477 bodies were buried here, and if modern-day visitors to the cemetery appear puzzled as to how a small area could accommodate so many people, they have every right to be. Today's El Campo Santo is smaller than it used to be: its grounds once spanned as far as Old Town Avenue, and roads and small businesses have been built over where the dead lay buried.

In 1889 a horse-drawn streetcar line was built through the cemetery. The line eventually became San Diego Avenue and when it was finally paved in 1942, rumors spread that as many as 18 bodies were left where they lay beneath the street and sidewalk. It was a little shocking for the San Diego Historical Society to hear, since it began restoration efforts at El Campo Santo as early as 1933 to reverse years of neglect and deterioration. The society relied upon early photographs and records to reset grave markers and reconstruct enclosures as best as they could. They also placed a white cross at the cemetery's center. But the damage had been done, and whispers began of ghosts and spirits walking the cemetery and its surroundings.

People working at the nearby Whaley House began seeing the apparition of a man they believed to be Yankee Jim Robinson. It was shocking, to be sure, since Robinson had been hanged on the grounds in 1852 after being found guilty in the theft of a rowboat in a farcical trial during which little concrete evidence had been presented. Robinson's death was particularly gruesome. His neck did not break as it should have when he was hanged. Instead, Robinson dangled from his noose for close to half an hour as the life was being ever slowly choked from his body. But now it appeared as if something had disturbed the alleged criminal from his resting-place in El Campo Santo Cemetery. Could it have been the way city planners had disturbed the sanctity of El Campo Santo when they began paving over the dead? No one will ever know for certain, but many people believed that El Campo Santo Cemetery is home to a host of ghosts who have helped make it one of California's most vibrant historic sites.

The ghosts have been embraced by the community and are often the highlight of walking tours through San Diego's Old Town. Guides clad in costumes often lead the way, pointing out where and which ghosts have been seen.

Tobias Buckley (an alias) loves history. It's what he's studying at a Big Ten school in the Midwest. After he's finished, he plans to get his doctorate in the field. For Buckley, history comes alive when he's conducting research and when he visits historical sites.

A palpable history. A tangible history. It's what brought Buckley to San Diego. That and the fact that he was visiting a brother who had moved out west long ago. Buckley fell in love with the city as he explored along the Pacific Coast Highway. But it was Old Town that captured his imagination. As he walked its streets, he found that it was still quite easy to cast his mind back to a time when paved roads were just a vision of the future, when paths were carved not by rubber, but by hooves and wooden wheels.

As he walked down San Diego Avenue, his attention was drawn to the little cemetery on the 2400 block of the street. Scattered at the gnarled roots of majestic olive trees were dozens of simple white crosses, many of them enclosed with white picket fences. Cacti dotted the grounds and the olive trees bent their leafy heads in the wind, swaying along with the palm trees so commonly associated with San Diego. A low adobe wall ran along the enclosure and Buckley found himself transfixed.

"It doesn't look like your typical cemetery," he says. "It was simpler and small. Very very small. And surrounded by traffic and the commotion of everyday life. It was a strange juxtaposition—you've got the living on one side, going about their business, and the dead on the other, whose business was concluded so long ago."

Intrigued by what he saw, Buckley returned the following day. He parked his rental car alongside the adobe wall of El Campo Santo Cemetery. It was night. There was a light cooling breeze that scoured the air of its daytime mugginess. He stood quietly at the cemetery wall and lost himself in the glowing candles that feebly lit the graves beyond. Shadows played across the small enclosures and it looked very different indeed to him than it had the day before. The effect of the candles was eerie, but it was something else. There was something more tangible about the chill that was beginning to creep along Buckley's spine.

"Yeah, it was very bizarre. I just suddenly felt very cold," he says. "And it was a very warm night. It is San Diego, after all." Still, Buckley proceeded along to the cemetery's entrance, where he was greeted by a costumed tour guide. A few others filled out the group and as they walked through the cemetery, they were regaled with stories about Antonio Garra, who attempted to lead a confederation of natives in driving Americans from California but was executed for his efforts, and Yankee Jim Robinson and others who most likely had had the misfortune of being in the wrong place at the wrong time only to encounter frontier justice. Buckley found the tour fascinating, but a little sanitized.

Of course, Buckley was also careful to point out that if everyone had the experience that he did at El Campo Santo, then there wouldn't be a need for costumed tour guides. At various points in the cemetery, Buckley was overwhelmed by a presence time and time again.

The tour was over and the cemetery quickly emptied, but Buckley was in no hurry to leave. He walked San Diego Avenue, up and down Arista and Conde, before returning to the cemetery where he had parked his car. He was just about to enter his rental car when something along the sidewalk caught his attention.

"I thought the cemetery was closed," he says, "but then there I am, standing on the sidewalk, and this figure is approaching me. And he's dressed up in period costume and I'm thinking, 'Oh, maybe he forgot something.'"

The figure continued to approach and it was then that Buckley noticed that there was something a little off about the man. He seemed translucent, almost as if he were a three-dimensional image projected onto the sidewalk.

"He seemed a little fuzzy," Buckley describes, "around the edges. Like someone had taken an eraser to his outline." Buckley remembered waving at the figure, but received no response. The man just walked by Buckley and then disappeared.

"One minute he was there," Buckley recalls, "the next, well, he wasn't. He just faded from existence into nothingness. I've never seen anything like it. I've got no idea who it could be. Maybe it was a long dead tour guide who just can't give up the ghost? Or maybe it was someone unhappy that his grave was paved over and made into a street?"

Buckley stared at the spot where he'd seen the apparition vanish, almost as it would magically bring the figure back. His mind raced with all sorts of questions, but there was no one around to answer them for him. Had he really just seen a ghost? Or was he hallucinating? He couldn't be sure.

Buckley looked up and down the street to see if anyone else had seen what he'd witnessed and though the avenue was relatively busy, with groups of two or three people walking down the sidewalk, none of them seemed particularly perturbed. He must have looked strange just standing there because a group of three men stopped in front of him.

"You having car trouble?" one of the men asked.

Buckley thought it an odd question. Puzzled, he just turned to the man and said, "No, I don't think so."

"Just making sure," the man said. "You looked a little confused, just standing there and staring off into space. I've seen it a lot around here. Especially right here by this cemetery."

Buckley was suddenly intrigued. "What do you mean?"

"Oh," the man continued, pointing into the cemetery, "it all goes back to that place. Strange stuff goes on in there. I've heard all the stories. But I always see people like you, just standing and staring, like they don't know if they're coming or going. And usually, it's got something to do with El Campo Santo."

Buckley nodded in understanding. "Well, sir, I am just such a person. And it has everything to do with El Campo Santo." He described what he had seen and the stranger just nodded.

"Yeah," the man said. "You saw a ghost, all right. You weren't the first and well, as sure as you and I are standing here, you won't be the last. You have yourself a good night."

Buckley waved goodbye and watched as the man turned to catch up with his friends. But then, the man stopped and came back.

"There's just one more thing, if your car doesn't start. I wouldn't worry about it. Just wait and try it again. It'll be fine."

Buckley stared quizzically at the stranger.

The stranger saw the question in Buckley's eyes and continued. "You'll see what I'm talking about. You've parked your car on top of the dead. Seems they don't like it, and they keep cars from starting. Every now and then, they'll set off the car alarms. It makes quite the racket. You take care now."

"It was definitely not an ordinary night," Buckley says. "But still, I was happy to hear that I wasn't completely crazy."

As for his car, Buckley realized within seconds of the man's exit that he spoke the truth. He inserted his key into the ignition and turned the key. Nothing happened. Not even a whirring sound or a sputter. Just the click of the key turning and then silence. Buckley sighed. Despite what the man had said, Buckley still wanted to find a rational explanation. His car wouldn't start, not because of some ghosts, but because the battery had died. He popped the hood of the car and got out to take a look at the engine. Everything appeared to be in place.

"It didn't take too long. I think I waited maybe about 10, 15 minutes," Buckley recalls. "By that time, I just wanted to go back to my brother's. I'd had enough of ghosts for one night." Buckley drove back to his brother's and recounted the tale over highballs of scotch. His brother took the story all in stride and could barely conceal his laughter.

"Yeah," Buckley says, "he knew exactly what happened down at El Campo Santo. He thought it would be funny not to warn me about the ghosts and see what would happen. It was certainly a mind-opening experience, I'll say that much."

Buckley returned to the Midwest to finish his studies. Every now and then, he'll recall in stunning and vivid detail the chill he felt walking into the cemetery and through its markers. And whenever his car doesn't start, which happens often now in his 16-year-old car, he catches himself wondering if the defect is mechanical in nature or paranormal.

In February 2003, the California Society for Ghost Research, based in Corona, California, descended upon San Diego to investigate El Campo Santo Cemetery. They traveled throughout the southwestern United States seeking out the eerie and the strange, meticulously and methodically documenting whatever they could find and capture with their field equipment. Included among their equipment are EMF detectors, Geiger counters and IR thermometers.

Chad Patterson, founder of the California Society for Ghost Research, has always had an interest in ghosts, one that began when he was just a toddler.

"As a child," Patterson writes, "I remember my grandmother's house being haunted. My interest first involved collecting articles and any sort of personal note-gathering or research I could do on my own." But once Patterson became a teenager, he began visiting the sites and houses that he had read about as a child, eager to discover, for himself, the paranormal.

Passionate though Patterson was, he knew little about the investigative and research methods applied to paranormal research. "I knew nothing of tools of the trade, such as EMF detectors and Geiger counters. All I possessed were 'burning questions, an open mind and a flashlight.'"

He found others as driven and passionate about the work as he was and joined various paranormal research societies, finding kinship and inspiration within these communities. He was co-director of the San Gabriel Valley Paranormal Researchers and was involved with the Orange County Society for Psychic Research before forming the California Society for Ghost Research in the last few years. To this date, Patterson has now conducted investigations of close to 100 sites, including hotels, cemeteries, museums, private houses, landmarks and other historical sites.

Patterson first read about El Campo Santo Cemetery on a visit to the Old Town district of San Diego in 1999. He has investigated the site most recently in 2003.

The day in February was relatively mild, with just a few wisps of cloud in the sky. Patterson led the investigation and was accompanied by Tracy Austin, Dede Miller, Nancy Richling, Alma Englesman, Jose Marco, George Austin and a psychic, Virginia Marco. The team came ready, toting two EMF detectors, an IR thermometer, a video camera and a variety of cameras.

Patterson began the investigation by walking through the cemetery with an EMF detector. The readings were surprisingly normal, indicating the presence of nothing more unusual than the expected background radiation. He did, however, see something strange in a place near the middle of the cemetery. This reading was not altogether unexpected either.

One of the psychics with whom Patterson works, Virginia Marco, felt something in the area. There was no visible spirit, but the EMF readings coupled with the tingling everyone seemed to be experiencing within their fingertips seemed to support Marco's intuitions. According to the psychic, the spirit of a small boy was trapped in the cemetery for reasons that she couldn't quite discern. She sensed within him great confusion, but nothing more. The boy never did materialize and Patterson suspected that the boy's spirit was weak; after all, it takes a "tremendous amount of energy for materialization." Marco did her best to comfort the trapped spirit before exorcising him, but she still sensed something else lurking.

Somewhere within the small and tidy cemetery was another ghost. Curious, Patterson asked Marco to elaborate and it was her opinion that El Campo Santo Cemetery was often visited by the ghost of a gravedigger. It was an intriguing development. Many ghosts had been seen at El Campo Santo Cemetery over the years, including a woman in a white Victorian dress, a Hispanic or Native American who hovers just above the ground and the misty glowing figure just outside the cemetery wall. Despite the countless sightings, these ghosts remained completely anonymous. No one seemed to know who they might have been in life or, more importantly, what had happened to trap them on the corporeal plane. Patterson speculated that the gravedigger was Rafael Mumudes who once worked at El Campo Santo Cemetery.

In the end, it was the psychic's opinion that the cemetery might have once been the site of a number of active hauntings but that their busiest days were long behind them. She could sense little to suggest otherwise. Marco even discredited the existence of El Campo Santo Cemetery's most famous ghost, that of Yankee Jim Robinson. While his spirit has allegedly been seen both at El Campo Santo and, more commonly, at the Whaley House, Marco was fully convinced that "Yankee Jim does not haunt El Campo Santo Cemetery, nor [even] the Whaley House."

Patterson's investigation lasted just over an hour and a half. Although the news that El Campo Santo Cemetery was not quite the haunt that it used to be might be dispiriting to some, Patterson was guided by a dogged pursuit of the truth. Rather than focusing on the legends and the sensational, he has chosen instead to emphasize the mundane. It is all part of his quest to legitimize his chosen field. What caused the hauntings and then what caused them to stop? Patterson pointed to the year 1993 as the time when the ghosts of El Campo Santo were quieted.

"I think, perhaps," he writes, "that recognition of the bodies may have something to do with the decrease in activity. I've heard stories that the cemetery might have been exorcised, but I have no evidence that this was ever done."

Outside of El Campo Santo Cemetery, there are two plaques. Inscribed upon them are memorials to those forgotten bodies that were lost to history when an old horse-drawn path was paved and became San Diego Avenue. In 1993, people in San Diego were all too familiar with the story that bodies had been left where they lay, that graves had been paved over with asphalt. Some were understandably outraged. It's an odd thing to picture, descendants of the dead reflecting upon loved ones as they stand not in a cemetery, but just outside, in the middle of a road while inciting the ire of motorists. While removing San Diego Avenue was not viable, it was decided that ground-penetrating radar would be used instead to settle once and for ever exactly how many bodies were buried beneath the street. They found more than 20 lying beneath San Diego Avenue and the remains of 13 people, mostly children, in an area behind the cemetery. The story was inscribed upon the plaques and while the plaques may seem woefully inadequate to atone for years of neglect, it just might have been enough to quell some of the restless dead.

Patterson admits that he can't be entirely sure what caused the hauntings, but hypothesizes that "much of the reported paranormal activity, at its peak several years ago, was due to the shrinking boundaries of the cemetery as graves were built and paved over." He seems a little more confident in saying that before 1993, El Campo Santo Cemetery was home to a number of spirits. There are too many accounts to dismiss and even though El Campo Santo may not be as haunted it once may have been, it is still a tangible and very real connection to San Diego's long and storied past.

For Patterson, El Campo Santo Cemetery is just another step towards proving the existence of the paranormal, which is his ultimate goal. "Once science has a more efficient means to study, the paranormal will receive the legitimate attention it deserves. We're merely scraping the surface at present...science is discovery. It will continue to make leaps and bounds. I feel many will not accept the paranormal until they are able to see, hear, smell, taste and touch it for themselves."

Gypsies Cemetery

CROWN POINT, INDIANA

Crown Point, Indiana, is home to the Gypsies Cemetery, the final resting place of an ostracized people who gained in death what they could not achieve in life. Located on a stretch of land that is now called Nine Mile, the small wooded lot dates back to the early 19th century. It draws its origins from a time when individuals who appeared different found themselves pushed to the fringes of society.

As its name implies, the cemetery was founded by a band of gypsies. In 1820, these gypsies, because of trouble with the local townspeople, were expelled from the town of Crown Point. Soon after, they fell victim to an outbreak of influenza. The townspeople refused them medical treatment and supplies, and the harsh winter conditions made recovery all the more difficult.

At the end of the winter, when the last of the snows had melted, the townspeople set out to see whether the unwelcome visitors had departed Nine Mile, taking the dreaded epidemic with them. The gypsies had indeed moved on, but they had left their dead behind. The land was marked with burial mounds and makeshift tombstones.

Some say that in doing so, the gypsies, so poorly treated by the townspeople, left a curse on the area. Others dismiss this idea, as the townspeople soon used the cemetery as one of their own.

The question of whether there is a curse in the region does not seem to trouble the minds of the local populace.

By all accounts, the Gypsies Cemetery has become a popular place, especially at Halloween. Over the last several
years, many residents have visited the site. And most of
those have reported strange events and happenings.

One story says that should a Bible be brought to the
graveyard, the book will start burning. Another states that
the bottoms of the pants of people walking over the
grounds will turn red, as if the wearer had walked through
blood. Less extreme rumors are about the occurrence of
strange smells, areas of sudden warmth or chill and glowing orbs of light making their way across the night sky.

People walking near the burial ground have also
reported a light from a mysterious campfire illuminating
the stands of trees and tombstones like some eerie jack-o-
lantern. Of course, when these people moved in for a
closer look, the light vanished. The same happened for
those who drove by in their cars. When the drivers
glanced in their rearview mirrors, they saw blue balls of
light following them. But when they stepped out to investigate, not a trace of the spectral illuminations remained.

Whether or not there is a curse from the gypsies who
abandoned the graveyard so many years ago is unknown,
but there is definitely something unnatural and unusual
about the area. Fortunately, the people of Crown Point
seem to have embraced rather than rejected their encounters with the supernatural.

Who knows what the gypsies might have to say about
this turn of events? They may have been banished in life,
but they appear to have gained acceptance in death.

Drummond Hill Cemetery

NIAGARA FALLS, ONTARIO

Once, a long time ago, Drummond Hill Cemetery was a tourist attraction that rivaled even the overwhelming popularity of Niagara Falls. Located south of Lundy's Lane, between Portage Road and Drummond Road, the Drummond Hill Cemetery benefited greatly from its proximity to Niagara Falls, although its appeal lay not with nature's wonder, but with history. The cemetery itself is old, with tombstones dating back to the closing years of the 18th century. Given its age, it's no surprise that Drummond Hill Cemetery is bursting with historical significance. It was at Drummond Hill Cemetery where the Battle of Lundy's Lane was fought.

The War of 1812 was a conflict between the United States and the United Kingdom that lasted for almost three years. The war was driven by an American desire to annex the British colonies in North America and fulfill its dream of westward expansion. Britain, of course, did not take to the idea. The Canadian colonies were still British, after all, and Britain still had its own interests to protect on the North American continent. The United States declared war on June 18, 1812.

Both sides were ill equipped, originally, for the conflict. Britain was in the midst of the Napoleonic Wars, while the United States' army was poorly trained, undermanned and woefully disorganized. The Americans also assumed that the Canadian colonies, so far removed from

British reinforcements, would be easily overrun. They were mistaken. In fact, once Napoleon's army had been defeated by the Russian winter in 1812, Great Britain was able to bring more pressure upon the United States. In 1814, British forces burned Washington, the White House was torched and President James Madison fled the city, deflating American morale.

For Canadians, the war had effectively ended earlier that year, after it had seemed as if the tide had turned against Upper and Lower Canada. American generals, like Winfield Scott, realizing how ill prepared their men had been in the campaigns of 1813, began drastically improving the skills and discipline of the army. The tactic worked and the American army was no longer subject to the failures and tactical errors that had condemned so many of its expeditions the year before.

The war had killed thousands, but neither side made territorial concessions. British and Canadians viewed the war as an American defeat for the American troops had been repulsed at the Canadian border twice: once in 1813 and again in 1814, at Lundy's Lane. Americans believed that they had successfully defended their rights and established the United States as a global power, able to resist the strength and might of Great Britain. For Canadians, the conflict created a sense of nationalism that had not existed before. The war finally culminated in peace with the signing of a treaty at Ghent on Christmas Eve, 1814. American President James Madison ratified it on February 17, 1815, bringing the conflict to its official end.

There is little doubt among Canadian historians that if it had not been for the War of 1812 and battles like that at

Drummond Hill Cemetery in Niagara Falls, Ontario

Lundy's Lane, Canada would have been easily absorbed into the United States. Drummond Hill Cemetery is then an important site, not just for those who are buried beneath its grounds and their descendants, but also for all Canadians.

Local folklore, as related by the Ontario Ghosts and Hauntings Research Society, holds that Drummond Hill Cemetery became popular with visitors when battle veterans, some of whom had decided to settle in the area, began offering impromptu tours of the battlegrounds.

Often, their accounts were tailored to the specifications of their audience, for the site appealed to Canadians, British and Americans alike.

Like tourists of the past who came to hear grizzled veterans tell their tales, tourists of the present come to see the same soldiers tell their stories. How is this seemingly impossible feat accomplished? Drummond Hill Cemetery, it turns out, is one of the most haunted cemeteries in all of Canada. Soldiers who fought in the Battle of Lundy's Lane patrol these fields still, trapped by the tragedy and devastation of a battle fought almost two centuries ago.

In July, General Winfield Scott began the American assault of the Niagara peninsula. Flush from a victory at the Battle of Chippewa, Scott, with an army of roughly 2000 men, invaded Canada at Niagara Falls, Upper Canada, on July 25, 1814. Sent to engage him was a hybrid army of 2000 British, Canadian and native soldiers, led by Sir Gordon Drummond. The British army had placed the brunt of their artillery atop a hill, just off Lundy's Lane and in and around the tombstones of Drummond Hill Cemetery. From this perch, it was a simple matter of firing down upon the American troops who emerged from the chestnut forest onto an open field below. The British army appeared to have a decided advantage. But the cannon that held the Americans at bay took too long to reload and it left the British artillery vulnerable to a counterattack. They held the higher ground, but American troops stormed the position and managed to wrest control of the cannon away from the British. For at least awhile. The battle had begun at about 7 PM and until night fell, momentum shifted one way and then the other, as armies gained, and then lost, control of Drummond Hill. With night's arrival, the battle descended into a kind of madness.

The night air was hot and muggy. Smoke from cannon and musket fire hung thickly in the air, shrouding the battlefield and effectively blinding both armies. With each shot fired, the smoke only grew thicker. Over tombstones and fences, the battle raged. Panic and fear had soldiers firing at anything that might look human through the smoke. Positions could only be marked with muzzle flashes and rockets and even then, the two armies still couldn't be sure whether or not they were firing upon the enemy or their own men. Casualties mounted on both sides, but the armies did not realize the extent of the devastation until dawn, when the thick smoke from gunfire had finally lifted.

As midnight approached, the two armies had fought themselves to a standstill. The British were at an advantage. As the defenders, they only had to break the will of the Americans to fight. The Americans, on the other hand, had to defeat their enemy soundly. With casualties mounting, General Winfield Scott appraised the situation. He saw that his supply lines were overextended and realized that he no longer had the men necessary to hold the higher ground. Early in the morning of July 26, Scott sounded the retreat. The British army nearly collapsed in sheer exhaustion and spent what little remained of the night slumbering amidst the tombstones and the fallen at Drummond Hill.

As for the Americans, they retreated back towards Chippewa, burned all bridges behind them so that the British couldn't harry them from the rear, torched Bridgewater Mills and fought and defeated a small British force at Fort Erie, Upper Canada. The British, Canadian and native soldiers were left to deal with the carnage.

Almost half of the men involved the battle had been killed, captured or wounded. Drummond Hill Presbyterian Church, a log structure set near the cemetery, lay in ruins. The American army claimed 860 casualties, while the British army claimed 878. The dead lay scattered across the grass, enemies and allies piled on top of each other in a sick embrace. They had fallen next to each other, so close had their firing lines been. The acrid smell of gunpowder hung closely to the nostrils and the field echoed with the screams of the wounded and dying for whom early 19th-century surgeons, with their saws and crude instruments, could do little. They had little time left to them before they too joined the dead in mass graves or the funeral pyre.

Both sides claimed victory. The battle had been one of the bloodiest ever fought on Canadian soil and represented the last invasion of Canada during the War of 1812 and, more importantly, the end of the United States' vision of uniting the whole of the North American continent beneath the Stars and Stripes.

The carnage of the Battle of Lundy's Lane also had a more local and direct impact. Tragedy has a way of trapping the dead and of psychically scarring the land; battlefields are notoriously haunted and Drummond Hill Cemetery is certainly no exception.

Ghosts of soldiers killed at the Battle of Lundy's Lane are said to haunt the grounds.

Once just a pastoral path that wended its way through southern Ontario, Lundy's Lane is now a major roadway. According to Matthew Didier, founder of the Ontario Ghosts and Hauntings Research Society, the cemetery "is a nice spot with tons of history, but it's not really all that restful. The thoroughfare Lundy's Lane makes up the northern border of the cemetery and...has quite a bit of traffic pretty much 24-7." A motel sits now at the bottom of the hill, while the rebuilt Drummond Hill Church rests next to the cemetery itself. The landscape has changed, but within the cemetery the past still beats with a pulse all its own. Indeed, as development began to work its way towards the cemetery, excavators, digging up the verdant fields to make room for houses and other buildings, uncovered what Didier called "the grisly relics" of the battle. The discoveries also added to the cemetery's growing reputation as one of the most haunted sites in all of Canada.

The cemetery itself is relatively small, spanning just four acres, spread out in basically a rectangle. Soaring trees, with their thick trunks and canopies of leaves, are scattered sparsely across the cemetery. Despite the traffic and the homes, it's still an uncluttered, well-kept place of reflection. There are monuments here, some dedicated to the War of 1812 itself, while others commemorate individuals who took part, such as Laura Secord. It's her statue that many claim has eyes that follow individuals making their way through the cemetery. The statue only adds to the eeriness of the place. It whets the appetite, arousing the curiosity with its promise of something more and something beyond the pale. And at Drummond Hill Cemetery, there is.

According to many ghost researchers and eyewitnesses, Drummond Hill Cemetery is haunted by not just one set, but two sets of different soldiers. When they appear, one might be fooled into thinking that reenactors have taken to the field. Of course, reenactors do not fade from the earth without a trace of their passing. One set is a troop of five soldiers, dressed in the uniform of the Royal Scots. They appear hurt, limping and lurching their way across the former battlefield. Once they've made their way towards the horizon, they fade from view. The other group is composed of three British soldiers, clad in their distinctive red uniforms, slowly making their way up the hill towards Drummond Hill Cemetery. Once there, they settle into a steady march before disappearing into the ether.

While the Ontario Ghost and Hauntings Research Society has written on the cemetery and is more than familiar with the accounts of Drummond Hill Cemetery, the society has yet to conduct a complete and thorough investigation of the site.

The society is the creation of Matthew James Didier. Didier wasn't always interested in the paranormal world. Before 1985, his interests lay more with aliens and extraterrestrials than with ghosts and wraiths.

"Up until that time," Didier writes, "my parents should have been more worried about their son becoming a UFOlogist rather than a ghost researcher." But in 1985, Didier had an epiphany. He doesn't describe exactly what he saw or what might have happened, but it's safe and easy to assume that it had something to do with the paranormal.

"Once I had experienced something" Didier writes, "I was hooked to looking into ghosts, their study and the phenomena forever. The more I read, the more I wanted to know." When Didier founded the Ghosts and Hauntings Research Society in 1997, he was surprised at the lack of websites devoted to ghosts in Canada.

"I found four sites," he recalls. "Three in the US and one, selling books, in Canada." Didier was determined to fill the void and to do so guided with his philosophy: to tell a story first and offer the proof second with thorough research supporting both. Ghosts aren't just simply orbs and mysterious noises in the night; they are a piece of history, a part of folklore. In essence, they are a part of ourselves and to study them is to study our own humanity.

"The study [of ghosts] is more than simply a good scare or a weird photo or two," he writes. "It's a chance to get people interested in history and folklore." Indeed, it is most assuredly the folklore and history that render each ghost unique and original.

Interestingly enough, Didier, even after years of seeking out the paranormal, still considers himself a "true skeptic," someone who hasn't dismissed the idea that ghosts do exist but who also isn't willing to take things on blind faith. He demands evidence before he believes, dismissing long-held assumptions and beliefs about psychical phenomena. It's an approach that has won him some supporters as well as detractors, both within and outside of the field of paranormal research. Of course, in a field that is still struggling for legitimacy and acceptance, it's not surprising that so many people have developed theories and ideas and practices about the paranormal. Like most individuals, Didier does what he believes to be correct. He laughs off his critics, pointing that he would never even deign to call himself a parapsychologist or an expert.

"I'm a well read and experienced researcher at best," he says. "My hope is that one day, I might get tapped to establish a parapsychology course for an accredited, postsecondary educational facility." Until then, Didier continues to work as a computer technician by day and a ghost researcher whenever he can.

Didier has yet to formally investigate the Drummond Hill Cemetery, but he has taken a number of trips to the site to take photos and perform what he calls "a *comme ça* investigation." He can't remember exactly when he first heard about the Battle of Lundy's Lane, but he feels as if he's always known about it and its hauntings.

Unfortunately, Didier has never "seen, heard, felt or experienced anything that could be perceived to be paranormal in the cemetery" but allows that "there are several excellent witness accounts so [the hauntings] can't be discounted." He points to Lundy's Lane and its traffic as one reason why it's difficult to carry out a thorough investigation of the site.

"There's so much ambient noise," Didier laments, "it would be difficult to get proper readings. Also, the ghosts of the soldiers are seen rather infrequently, making a sighting highly unlikely, though not impossible." Impediments, to be sure, but a number of other paranormal research groups have investigated the site and come up with their own peculiar results.

One of these groups, the Western New York Ghosts and Hauntings Society, is actually affiliated with Didier's organization, falling under the umbrella of the Organization of Ghosts and Hauntings Research Societies, of which Didier's was the first. Formed in December 2002, the Western New York Ghosts and Hauntings Society came to Niagara Falls in March 2003. Although society member Pete Sexton had no plans to investigate Drummond Hill Cemetery, he and members of Burlington Ghost Research and the Paranormal and Ghost Society somehow ended up on its grounds.

Sexton began his night at about 10 PM, when he met his friends at the Flying Saucer Restaurant on Lundy's

Lane. Sexton and his friends discussed the wartime history of Niagara Falls and the bloody Battle of Lundy's Lane. Afterwards, he and the others wandered over to a Ramada Inn that had recently been built near the Drummond Hill Cemetery.

"From my understanding," Sexton writes on his website, "[the Ramada Inn] was erected on part of the battlefield." It seemed as good a place as any to look for the paranormal. They walked through the hotel and it was in one hallway that Sexton noticed something peculiar.

"I discounted the warm and cold spots," Sexton describes, "because of the heating system in the hotel. The placement of the windows and heating vents created natural warm and cold spots." But there was something more in the hallway that night and it perfumed the air.

Sexton could smell something and it certainly wasn't an odor common to sanitized hotel hallways and their customary floral scents.

"There was a strong smell of black powder smoke," Sexton writes. What was even more peculiar was how the scent varied in intensity as they moved through the hallway. It was strong one moment, faint and almost non-existent the next, leaving Sexton with little doubt in his mind that that particular hallway in the Ramada Inn was haunted.

From the Ramada, Sexton and the group turned towards Drummond Hill Cemetery. Even in the darkness, he still found the cemetery a lovely place, with "very old crypts and beautiful stones." They walked through the grounds, ever watchful for anything strange and unusual. They saw and heard nothing. And, in true narrative

The cemetery's atmosphere and haunted reputation have drawn several teams of paranormal investigators.

fashion, Sexton and his friends were almost ready to leave the cemetery when someone called them over to look at something on his digital camera.

Huddled around the small LCD screen of the camera, Sexton watched with awe. Though the image was tiny and blurry, Sexton could easily see what it was that had caught the cameraman's attention.

"In the view screen," Sexton writes, "there was ball of dancing blue light. Even with the camera set steady on a stone, the light moved left and right, up and down." Sexton looked from the screen to the cemetery, trying to see if there was a source of light that might be behind what they were all seeing. But the cemetery was bathed in darkness. The dancing ball of blue light existed only on the digital camera's screen and continued to play across the screen until Sexton and the group finally left the cemetery at 1 AM. While Sexton doesn't offer an explanation for what the light might have been, it's clear that the orb represented the paranormal and that Drummond Hill Cemetery was still home to restless spirits. Considering that Sexton hadn't planned on investigating the cemetery, he was thrilled that someone had brought along the digital camera. Neil Chartrand (an alias) didn't have a digital camera, but he did have a camcorder and the camcorder captured the bizarre event just as effectively as the digital camera had.

Not long ago, Neil, along with some friends from his high school, decided to pay a late night visit to Drummond Hill Cemetery. They were a little nervous about being in the place so late at night. It was a creepy place and Chartrand and his friends couldn't be sure whether or not they were trespassing. Of course, the idea that they were doing something illicit only made the trip all the more difficult to resist and they entered the cemetery, armed with their flashlights and camcorder. Their hearts beat heavily with anticipation.

"The minute we entered," Chartrand says, "I felt something in the pit of my stomach. I don't know if it was nerves or something, but I've never experienced anything like it. I was anxious, my palms were sweaty...it really felt like we were intruding or interrupting something."

A thin drizzle of rain fell from the skies and all of it combined to create an eerie and strange atmosphere. Tombstones, soaked with rain, glistened in the dark whenever the moon managed to peek out from behind the clouds. The trees cast sweeping shadows down upon Chartrand and his friends. They looked behind them repeatedly, worried that someone might have seen them enter the cemetery and would call the police in a panic.

But once they moved deeper into the cemetery, they allowed themselves to relax. Just a little. Unfortunately, the anxiety that he was being watched did not leave Chartrand.

"It only got worse the further I got into the cemetery," he remembers. "I wanted to leave but we'd walked quite a way to get to Drummond Hill and well, nobody wants to look like a chicken."

Chartrand kept quiet, relieved to learn later that his friends had been just as uneasy as he had been. For the time being, however, he kept telling himself that it was just nerves. In one hand, he held his flashlight. He played the beam around him, illuminating dozens of tombstones at once.

"I didn't realize there were so many," he says. "But there they were...just scattered across the ground." He and his friends peered at the dates on the stones, marveling at their age and feeling, perhaps for the first time, the inexorable weight of history.

Chartrand, like Matthew James Didier, doesn't remember when he first learned of the ghosts at Drummond Hill

Cemetery. They were out to see the ghostly troop of marching soldiers for themselves and had brought along the camcorder to record the moment.

They wandered the cemetery, walking among the tombstones, watching and waiting for something—anything—to happen. Nothing did. Then Chartrand remembered something he had read. He recalled reading an article about Drummond Hill Cemetery and how people had taken strange photos at the place. Orbs or ecto-mist would appear in one or two photos in a sequence of many, and were acknowledged, though not universally, as proof of the paranormal. They hadn't brought a camera with them, but they did have the camcorder.

"I told my friend to turn it on," Chartrand says, "hoping that we might see something strange on the camcorder."

His friend, somewhat skeptical and a little reluctant to use the camcorder in the rain, finally relented. He turned it on and almost immediately, he noticed something wholly bizarre.

"It was the weirdest thing," Chartrand recalls. "It was like the camcorder had a mind of its own. It just started zooming in and out of focus. We thought at first that he didn't know what he was doing. But it became pretty clear this wasn't the case. The thing did have autofocus, but even when we turned it off, the darn thing kept zooming in and out."

Even more puzzling was how the camcorder would behave differently if it was pointed at different areas of the cemetery. There were areas where it would even lose focus completely, with nothing but a blurry haze on the viewfinder. While watching the images, Chartrand became aware of a chill that was beginning to settle into his bones, even though the night was warm and humid.

While walking back to Chartrand's house, the group brought the camcorder out one more time. They wanted to see whether or not the camcorder was defective or if the interference they'd seen was truly the work of the paranormal. The camcorder, now safely outside of the cemetery, operated perfectly. The autofocus worked fine, as did the zoom. Whatever had taken control of the device was now leaving it alone.

Chartrand and his friends got together the next day to watch the footage they had shot. The images that had been clear and pristine the night before were rendered choppy and blurry, while the footage taken after they had left the cemetery was unmarred.

"I've got no explanation for what happened that night," Chartrand says. "All I can say is that cemetery is definitely a really strange place to be. I still watch that video every now and then and just shake my head. It's a great place, but it's definitely creepy. I'm not an expert or anything, but it's haunted in my eyes."

Chartrand, of course, is not the only individual to believe in Drummond Hill Cemetery's paranormal presences. The spirits, though they appear infrequently, have given every indication that they are still fighting the Battle of Lundy's Lane and will not rest anytime soon.

Bachelor's Grove

CHICAGO, ILLINOIS

It's a place that time seems to have forgotten. Overrun with vegetation and vandalized by trespassers, Bachelor's Grove Cemetery is a grim, desolate and ruined place. Tombstones lie scattered in pieces and the remains of animals, reportedly sacrificed to Satan, are strewn throughout the cemetery. It was once a place where people gathered near the adjacent quarry pond for picnics, or for a swim and some fishing. Now all that remains are memories of lives past and a host of ghosts who have turned Bachelor's Grove into one of the most haunted sites of Chicago, and also of the United States.

Even the origins of its name are uncertain. Some people believe that the grove was named for the Batchelder family. Settlement of this area, according to Tinley Park Historical Society president Brad L. Bettenhausen, began in the early 19th century with settlers arriving from New York, Vermont and Connecticut. By the mid-19th century, immigrants from Germany flocked to the area. Not only did these German families create a life for themselves out of the wilderness, they bestowed their family names to this new land to mark their legacy. Walker's Grove, then, was named for the Walker family. The same is true of Gooding's Grove and Cooper's Grove. Records show that the Batchelder family had already immigrated to Illinois by 1845 and would have likely followed the tradition others had established.

Others believed that Bachelor's Grove was named not for a family, but for a group of German men who lived on this stretch of terrain along Lake Michigan as they worked on digging the Illinois-Michigan Canal. Many of the men were single—bachelors essentially—and it was in their honor that Bachelor's Grove was named.

Confusion aside, Bachelor's Grove is one of the oldest cemeteries in Illinois' Cook County, located just across from the Rubio Woods Forest Preserve, at the end of a littered stretch of road that once was a part of the old Midlothian Turnpike. The first person was buried at Bachelor's Grove in November 1844. The cemetery was officially closed in 1965, and the access road was later closed to traffic.

Hidden and isolated, Bachelor's Grove Cemetery became popular with teenagers on the lookout for a good party. The chain-link fence set around the cemetery was pried open, and teenagers acted with reckless abandon, defacing, breaking and stealing tombstones. Many of the tombstones were tossed into the quarry pond, which was also reportedly once a favorite dumping site of Chicago's infamous Mafia syndicate. In their place, partygoers left a litter of beer cans, cigarette butts and other debris. The cemetery also attracted those with a fascination with death, namely occultists and Satanists. On these hallowed grounds, they performed rituals involving animal sacrifice and the opening and robbing of graves. The descendants of many of those buried at Bachelor's Grove moved the bodies of their ancestors to active cemeteries, where the gravesites could be protected and maintained. The abandonment of Bachelor's Grove was nearly complete.

By the late 1970s, locals with a vested interest in Chicago's history sought to reverse the years of neglect and abuse. The Cook County Board was petitioned to assume responsibility for the cemetery, with the help of the Cook County Forest Preserve District. Now, the cemetery closes as soon as the sun has set and is patrolled by the Chicago Police Department and the Rubio Woods Forest Preserve. The mission of the Bachelor's Grove Restoration Project is to restore and preserve the cemetery and still the hands of vandals. Ghosthunters continue to prowl its grounds, seeking out proof for the countless spirits that allegedly haunt the cemetery.

Yes, Bachelor's Grove seems to have a diverse and stunning array of ghosts. Over the years, there have been hundreds, if not thousands, of sightings. Strange orbs of red and blue lights arc their way across the cemetery, an ethereal backdrop for the ghostly personae. Most of the spirits have been identified, though few people refer to them by their proper names. Instead, the spirits of Bachelor's Grove have been given pulpy but commonplace and mysterious names such as "the White Lady," "the Phantom Farmhouse," "the Two-Headed Creature from the Lagoon" and "the Farmer and his Horse."

Along the old road, witnesses have reported seeing what could only be a mirage: a white farmhouse, its many windows illuminated from within, turning its porch columns and swing into silhouettes. The structure is never static and it always disappears when approached. Even odder is that no such structure was ever built near the cemetery. And though the old road is no longer used, its closure means little to one driver in a black Prohibition-era sedan that continues to roar down the path. It has run through more than one pedestrian, but has yet to claim a victim. Instead, it simply passes through all corporeal matter, leaving individuals shaken but unscathed.

The old quarry pond, once a tranquil setting for picnics has became a home of the mysterious two-headed spirit. No one knew exactly who or what the creature is, but it is a truly frightening apparition that has blanched the face of more than one individual.

A far less terrifying quarry pond apparition was that of the Farmer and his Horse. In the 1870s, when land in Cook County was still being tilled and sown, a farmer plowing his field had steered his horse too closely to the pond. The horse stumbled into the waters, dragging behind him the farmer and the plow. The plow's weight proved too much for the wriggling and struggling horse to overcome and the farmer became hopelessly ensnared in the reins and made the pond his watery grave. Over a century after their deaths, the farmer and his horse continue to appear at the pond's edge before tumbling, once again, to their deaths.

Of Bachelor's Grove's spirits, perhaps the most famous and celebrated is the White Lady. Many have seen her through the years. Her appearance coincides with the rising of a full moon, at which time she walks the cemetery grounds, her white dress glowing in the moon's spectral soft light. Sometimes, cradled within her arms is her baby. In death, the two have been reunited.

In the early 1990s, a photograph appeared in the pages of *The National Examiner*. Few took notice of the image, until it ran in the pages of the highly respected *Chicago*

Sun-Times. It was a somewhat blurry black and white picture of a sun-drenched dark-haired woman dressed in a white dress. Her hands were clasped between her outstretched legs as she stared off into the distance. While she was bathed in sunlight, she did not cast a shadow and her legs were almost translucent. It was a stark, mournful image. To many, it was photographic evidence of the paranormal.

The photograph was taken on August 10, 1991, during a Ghost Research Society investigation of Bachelor's Grove. Based out of Oak Lawn, Illinois, the Ghost Research Society was born in 1977 and boasted among its membership writers Dale Kaczmarek and Dennis William Hauck. It was created, according to the society's website (www.ghostresearch.org), to be a "clearinghouse for reports of ghosts, hauntings, poltergeist and life after death encounters...to research and investigate all reports that come their way including private homes and businesses." Over the years, the society, under president Kaczmarek, has conducted countless investigations. Among these, of course, was an examination of Bachelor's Grove.

On August 10, while standing near a tombstone, society researchers noticed that their equipment, which included an air ion counter and a tri-field EMF meter (used to detect changes in extremely weak static or natural electric and magnetic fields), were giving readings that indicated that a spirit might be nearby. It was then that member Jude Huff-Felz took out her 35-mm camera, loaded it with infrared black and white film and snapped a shot. When the photograph was developed, the society realized that they had captured an image of the famous

White Lady of Bachelor's Grove. It had to be a ghost; no one could recall having seen a woman sitting comfortably on the tombstone when the picture was taken.

Since that time, other investigations have been carried out at Bachelor's Grove with equally puzzling results. One researcher, Brian Roesch, visited the site in 1999 on a late November afternoon of a very cold and windy day, armed with an EMF meter. Over the course of his four-hour exploration, Roesch experienced cold spots in numerous places and heard unexplained and eerie sounds. When his photos were developed, he noticed that many of them were speckled with cloudy spots, otherwise known as orbs and which indicated a spirit's presence. To him, the place was undoubtedly haunted.

"Ghosts are made of electrical energy," he explains. "This energy is in all living things. Animals too. It's a fact that electrical energy can't be destroyed, so I believe that the energy picked up by my EMF meter is the energy left behind by beings that have died." At Bachelor's Grove, his EMF meter took some odd readings, leading Roesch to conclude that "an energy was close." He heard strange sounds, such as "voices, footsteps, heavy breathing and music," which all pointed to the presence of the paranormal.

Finally, there are reports that the ghost of a man prowls the grounds of Bachelor's Grove. He is not a purely malevolent spirit, but nor is he friendly or accommodating. He seems rather gruff, perhaps more than a little cranky that something or someone has disturbed him from the slumber of his afterlife. Encounters with this grumpy ghost are more than enough to satisfy the curiosities of those who come to Bachelor's Grove in search of the paranormal. Just ask Carol Green and Nick Ryder (names are aliases). Both of them have seen things that led them to swear that they would never return again to Bachelor's Grove.

Carol Green, then a high school student in Chicago, had grown up on a steady diet of ghost stories, told to her by her father, many of which were culled from Bachelor's Grove. She found them absolutely fascinating and never found it all that strange that her father would put her to bed with the eerie accounts instead of fairy tales and fables.

"Sure, they scared me. They really scared me and believe me, there were a lot of nights where I was tossing and turning. But I got used to it, like you do with anything, and I couldn't get enough," she says.

Remembering the stories that had haunted her imagination ever since she'd heard them, Carol drove to Bachelor's Grove as soon as she was old enough.

"I just had to see these things for myself," she says, her voice rising with excitement at the memory, "How couldn't I? I believed in these ghosts and I really wanted to see them."

Her first trip was far from memorable. She went one sunny afternoon after school and in the bright light of day, the cemetery bore little resemblance to the dark and twisted place she had envisioned as a child. Wriggling her way through the cemetery fence, she was aghast to see the piles of cigarette butts and beer bottles that littered the ground.

She picked her way through the scattered tombstones, hoping to see or hear anything and something. But sadly, all that she heard was the dull roar of traffic from the

Midlothian Turnpike and she saw nothing particularly eerie or paranormal.

"It was creepy, though," Carol recalls. "I couldn't shake this feeling in the pit of my stomach. It was like there was a stone in my gut. The minute I left, it was gone. That was pretty bizarre."

Carol returned several times after that, sometimes with her two best friends, sometimes alone, sneaking out late at night when her parents had already gone to sleep. But despite all the risks that Carol took to see for herself a genuine live spook, nothing happened until Carol's senior year of high school.

Carol returned one fall night with a couple of her closest friends. She had brought a camera with her, having read and heard that ghost researchers often did, hoping to capture the presence of orbs.

"There was something different," Carol said. "Something different from the other times I'd gone there. I'd always felt weird being at the cemetery, but this time, it just felt a lot colder than it should have and I felt like there was something heavy just lightly pushing down on me. It was a strange, a really strange sensation. I'm pretty sure my friends felt it too. We just looked at each and other and knew that something was going to happen." They were right.

The beam from their flashlight that had thus far only illuminated gravel and weeds suddenly revealed a figure standing right in the middle of the path. He was almost translucent, his flesh a wisp. His features, at first blurry, began to come into focus. His face was a study in concentration with its furrowed brows, tightly set jaw and steely eyes. His clothing was straight from another era when men wore suits and hats.

"To be honest," Carol said, "he looked like a gangster. Dark pinstripe suit, the fedora. My friends and I just stood there, staring at him. He had a magnetic stare and his eyes. It was like they were boring holes in us."

As jarring as the experience was, Carol managed to maintain enough of her composure to snap a couple of quick shots of the apparition. When her photographs were developed, Carol was not surprised to see that four of the pictures couldn't be processed. They were, of course, the four that she had shot of the ghost.

"The pictures were just pitch black. I've got pictures of the trail that night and of my friends and they came out just fine. But the pictures of that ghost—just nothing but pitch black," Carol said. "I asked the developer about it and he offered all these different reasons for it, but I know what happened. I really did see a ghost." The experience left Carol shaken and a little disturbed. The trip to Bachelor's Grove in 2001 was her last.

"I don't think I could ever go back. It was just too…" Carol's voice trailed off, unable to put into words the ghost's impact. "No, I just can't go back." Years may have passed since Carol encountered her first spirit at Bachelor's Grove but the memory of that night was still very clear.

Nick Ryder has never met Carol Green, but he wouldn't mind doing so.

"It'd be nice to meet someone, who understands a little, or a lot, of what I went through," he said, his voice full of the brawn typically associated with Chicago. Nick,

In spite of age and vandalism, a handful of spirits still inhabit
Bachelor's Grove Cemetery in Chicago.

unlike Carol, however, never was all that interested in the
paranormal.

"I didn't really believe in the whole thing, but I had
friends that did. And every now and then, they'd manage
to convince me to go out on that old Midlothian Turnpike
and go looking for their ghosts," he says. "Everyone knew
about that place. You'd go there just to check it out and see
what it was like."

It was a cemetery, after all, and Nick had always found
them a little eerie, haunted or not. But as eager as his

friends had been, they never saw anything or out of the ordinary. Ironically enough, it was the skeptic in the group, Nick, who underwent the experience.

"It was a hot night. Really hot and muggy," he says, when recalling that evening in the summer of 2002. "We were coming back from the bar when someone suggested that we go to Bachelor's Grove. We'd never been there at night, they kept saying. So I thought, yeah, why not? I really wasn't ready to go home yet."

It turned out that they weren't the only ones that night with the very same idea. As they approached the cemetery's fence, a group of people had just left. Asked if they had seen any ghosts, the group just glumly shook their heads and then shuffled off down the road. Slightly discouraged, Nick and his friends continued through the fence, careful to speak in hushed tones lest the policemen patrolling the cemetery grounds hear them.

Immediately, Nick noticed something strange. He could see his breath on the wind, which struck him as odd. But standing there, Nick felt a chill grip his body and he found himself shivering in 75°F temperatures.

"It was the strangest thing," Nick says. "It was like I'd stepped into a freezer. One minute I was sweating, the next, the beads of sweat seem like they're freezing to my forehead. And then, to make it all the more fun, something touches the back of my neck. Something cold, clammy and fleshy. And it stays there. I really started to freak out."

His friends seemed to think that he was playing some practical joke, making light of their passions and therefore paid little attention to his plight.

"I could feel the hand still," Nick says. "And then I saw my friends. They were pointing behind me and they were scared shi—well, I shouldn't say how scared they were but you can figure it out." Nick ran from the cemetery once the hand on his neck began to move down his back. His friends followed quickly; they were all too happy to leave.

"We ran and ran. But I mean, that just goes to show you that there's something there in Bachelor's Grove," he says. "None of us scare easily, I'll tell you that much."

But what had his friends seen?

Nick asked them and he remains happy that he never looked back. His friends had caught a glimpse of a ghost, dressed in the clothing of Prohibition-era mobsters. He had a thick jaw, eyes of steel and a deeply furrowed brow. No one seemed to know who the spirit might be, but they knew what he was not. He was definitely not pleased.

"Yeah, I don't think he wanted us there," Nick says. "And we got his message pretty clear. That hand on my neck—I don't know what was going to happen, but I really didn't want to stick around and find out."

Nick is now a firm believer in ghosts, but refuses to ever take another trip to Bachelor's Grove. He knows they're out there, but for now, Nick prefers to deal strictly with the living.

There is no doubt too that the ghosts of Bachelor's Grove will continue to fascinate as they have done for years. Perhaps if Bachelor's Grove were restored to its original condition, then the spirits within would finally find peace.

Christ Church Cemetery

ST. SIMONS ISLAND, GEORGIA

The history of St. Simons Island, like many of the earliest American colonies, is steeped in religion and conflict. The island is an idyllic spot buttressed between Georgia and the Atlantic Ocean. It overlooks St. Simons Sound, a waterway that meanders into Georgia and towards the once-great plantation cities of Savannah and Darien. Given its location, it is little wonder that Spanish and British armies fought often for its strategic location.

Inhabited by Muskogean tribes for thousands of years, St. Simons Island first fell victim to imperialism in the early 16th century when Catholic monks from Spain established missions to convert the indigenous population and to settle the land. In later years, the English arrived with James Oglethorpe. Under the command of General Oglethorpe, English armies defeated their Spanish counterparts in 1742 in a brutal battle, aptly named the Battle of Bloody Marsh.

It seems the ghosts of the past are never far away on St. Simons Island. Built in 1810, St. Simons Lighthouse—destroyed in 1861 by retreating Confederate soldiers and rebuilt again in 1872—continues to operate under the watch of the United States Coast Guard, one of the nation's longest continuously operating lighthouses. Fort Frederica, built in the latter years of the 18th century to protect Darien and Savannah from the Spanish, who at the time were in firm control of Florida, serves today as a window into its past as the centerpiece of a burgeoning riverfront community and all that stood between Georgia and the Spanish. Many majestic oak trees blanket the island; eerily, many of them are etched with human faces. Known as tree spirits, these haunting and elegiac faces are the legacy of skilled artists seeking to memorialize the hundreds of sailors who lost their lives at sea, aboard vessels hacked and carved out of St. Simons Island oak. The trees themselves, with their sagging branches and beards of wispy moss, seem near unable to bear the emotional weight of these mournful monuments.

James Oglethorpe had brought with him a group of devout Protestant settlers. The first church on the island, Christ Church at Frederica, was completed in 1820 on land that it continues to occupy today. When the church was nearly destroyed by Union troops during the Civil War, Christ Church was rebuilt as a tribute to one man's love for his wife, country and God.

In the 1870s, a young man named Anson Greene Phelps Dodge decided to pay a visit to St. Simons. Like many before him, Dodge was won over by the island's sun and he decided to stay. He became a member of Christ Church at Frederica. But since its near destruction, he was disappointed that the plantation house of Black Banks had served as the meeting place for Christ Church parish. The church should be rebuilt. But Dodge was recently married, and he had other matters to attend to.

With his wife, Ellen, Dodge embarked on a tour of the globe. While they were in India, tragedy struck. Ellen fell ill and died. Devastated, Dodge wearily returned to St. Simons Island bearing his dead wife. He longed to memorialize his wife, to create a legacy that would inspire future generations. What better way to remember his wife, he thought, than through rebuilding Christ Church?

Christ Church was resurrected, but with an unusual addition. Beneath the church, Ellen Dodge was entombed. Dodge himself died in 1898, his latter years spent in service of St. Simons Island. When he was buried in Christ Church Cemetery, he and Ellen were at long last reunited. Her body was moved and the two now lie side by side in a cemetery that encompasses two centuries of history.

According to local folklore, the spirits of two souls haunt Christ Church Cemetery and they speak of a love pure and true. Some of the particulars of this love story have been lost, but it is still as moving and poignant.

Long ago, when St. Simons Island was still a British colony, a boy and a girl met and fell in love. It was the sort of love that was timeless and passionate. Their courtship was brief; in time, with the blessings of both their families, the two were wed in a simple ceremony at the original Christ Church.

They came to know and to love each other's habits and eccentricities. The husband laughed at his wife when he learned how she hated the dark. He too had been afraid of the dark, but when he was a child his parents had often left a candle burning in his room, waiting patiently until he had drifted off to sleep before extinguishing the flame. With this memory in mind, he did the same for his wife, lighting a candle in the room when they went to bed and watching her until she fell asleep. He never told her (though later he wished he had), but there were nights when he spent hours just watching her sleep—the way her

Does a ghostly candle flame still appear at Christ Church Cemetery?

long raven tresses fell divinely across the pillow and the way she curled up under the covers.

For months, life continued in this way, but finally the couple could no longer escape the harshness of their colonial life. Disease cared little for how much love they held, and his wife soon fell ill.

Poultices and leeches were applied on her. Surgeons cut and bled her. But nothing seemed to work. She became pale and fragile. Madness took hold of her in her final days, and she spoke only gibberish that her husband desperately tried to decipher for any meaning. When at last she expired, her husband tried to convince himself that she had gone to a better place, that death was release from her suffering. She was buried in a simple ceremony in Christ Church Cemetery.

Islanders mourned, but could do little to ease the husband's suffering. He was inconsolable. At night, he stared, with tear-filled eyes, at the emptiness of his room, a candle burning slowly to its end next to him. He was haunted with dark thoughts, of his wife lying in the cold, dark ground.

He began taking a candle at night to his wife's grave. Though he couldn't have possibly known it then, so began the healing of his heart. Without fail, the husband brought a candle each and every night, sometimes leaving quickly, sometimes staying behind to talk. He did this every night until his death, when at long last he was reunited with his wife. He was buried next to her. Friends and family, though sad to lose him, knew that he had finally found happiness again. But habits are hard to break.

People passing by the cemetery late at night often saw a candle lit by the wife's grave. Thinking that someone was playing a prank, some people decided to watch the grave one evening. As night fell, the crowd gasped in awe as they watched a flame flicker to life just above the wife's grave.

Today, the flame still flickers to life on dark and quiet nights in Christ Church Cemetery. It still speaks to the passion the tragic couple shared. Those who witness the spectral light cannot help but be moved in this storied and idyllic place.

The Valley of the Kings

EGYPT

The Valley of the Kings is a desolate and barren place carved out of sun-bleached limestone mountains. It isn't a typical cemetery, with sagging tombstones and weathered stone angels, but it is quite possibly the world's most famous burial place.

History and myth permeate the Valley of the Kings. Tourists descend each year to view the wealth and riches hidden just beneath the surface. Its desolate nature was what first attracted the ancient Egyptian pharaohs to the area. The rulers of Egypt's 18th, 19th and 20th dynasties (except for Ahmose, the first king of the New Kingdom, who built himself a pyramid at Abydos) had seen what had happened to the tombs of their ancestors. The Old Kingdom's towering pyramids of Giza dominated the landscape on the flat sand along the Nile's west bank. They could be seen for miles, a beacon to thieves and political enemies who desecrated the sacred tombs. Thieves stole countless items that the ancient pharaohs needed for their journey to the afterlife. Fearful that their ancestors would be trapped in purgatory, the royal families sought a more secret location.

Near the New Kingdom capital of Thebes, which included what is modern-day Luxor, the pharaohs found what they were looking for. It was a long, dry, river valley, known today as *Biban el-Muluk* or "the gateway of the kings," bordered on either side with soaring cliffs of limestone. Access to the valley via just one entrance could be strictly regulated, while the surrounding mountains kept the place hidden from prying eyes. The location seemed to be a divine gift, as the mountain that rose above the valley floor bore a strong resemblance to the pyramids at Giza.

From 1500 BC until roughly 1000 BC, Egypt's pharaohs did away with the elaborate exteriors of the pyramids. Instead, winding and dark corridors were hewn out of the valley limestone meant to confuse tomb raiders. Deep within was a sunken chamber where the mummified body and his possessions—furniture, food, statues and jewels—were placed. The entrance of the actual tomb was then concealed to blend in with its surroundings.

The walls of the pharaohs' tombs were carved and painted to recount the legend of the sun-god, Re, and his journeys through the underworld. The walls were inscribed with passages from the sacred texts of the Book of the Dead, the Book of the Gates and the Book of the Underworld. These carvings and paintings were meant to ensure the king's safe passage into the afterlife.

Through the centuries, the tombs lay undisturbed, and it seemed as if the pharaohs had been wise to choose what they knew as the Place of Truth for their burial site. But under the weak rule of the 20th dynasty, the tombs fell prey once more to looters and thieves. Desperate to save these treasures, the priests entered the tombs, retrieved the mummified remains and some of their treasures and reburied them in two secret caches.

The burial site remained relatively undisturbed for centuries, though ancient Greeks and Romans were known to have visited the Valley of the Kings. It wasn't

Even today, Egypt's Valley of the Kings conceals secrets of the great pharaohs.

until the 1700s that explorers began seeking out the valley's riches, but few knew then just how extensive the treasures were.

In the early 19th century, archaeologists discovered the first cache of the royal mummies. The discovery of Seti I's tomb in 1817 by an Italian explorer, Giovanni Belzoni, began a rush of excavations in the area. It was the rebirth of the pharaohs; to speak the names of the dead was to make them live again, according to ancient Egyptian beliefs. Stories of cursed tombs invoked an awed fascination with the site, which has not waned even today.

The man most associated with the Valley of the Kings and its reported curses is archaeologist Howard Carter, who uncovered the tomb of the little-known boy king Tutankhamun in 1922. One of over 60 tombs discovered and relatively small, Tutankhamun's tomb is by far the most celebrated burial site in the Valley of the Kings.

Howard Carter was born in 1873 in the small but wealthy township of Kensington, London. From an early age, Carter was trained in drawing and painting to follow in the footsteps of his father, who earned a living drawing portraits of animals for locals. Carter showed little interest in the creatures that formed the bulk of his father's portfolio. Instead, he rather longed to escape from England and explore the world. The country that captivated his imagination was Egypt.

At 17, Carter paid his first visit to the country that he had read about in books. He traveled to Alexandria, where his artistic training proved highly beneficial. Hired as a draftsman for the Egyptian Exploration Fund, Carter began working at Bani Hassan, where he recorded mural scenes from the tombs of Middle Egyptian princes. Carter was fascinated with the work and would often sleep within the very tombs where he worked.

Trained by eminent archaeologists William Flinders Petrie and Gaston Maspero, Carter perfected his skills in excavations carried out at the temple of Queen Hatshepsut. At the age of 25, he was appointed the Inspector-General of Monuments of Upper Egypt. He held that post until a violent incident involving drunken French tourists and his archaeology site guards at Saqqara led to his dismissal. For the next year and a half, Carter worked as a water-color painter and as an antiquities dealer. It seemed that his days as a working archaeologist were at an end.

Carter may have lost his job, but the work he had done had not gone unnoticed. Carter had caught the eye of the 5th Earl of Carnarvon, George Edward Stanhope Molyneux Herbert.

Born in 1866, Carnarvon was 23 when he inherited the title as well as an immense fortune and a large estate in Berkshire, England. At 34, while recovering from an auto-mobile accident, Carnarvon became fascinated with Egyptologist Gaston Maspero's work and began his own exploration of the Egypt's tombs and burial sites. Carnarvon met Carter in 1907 and eventually hired him as his Supervisor of Excavations.

In a scant five years, Carter discovered three royal tombs in the Valley of the Kings and endowed Carnarvon with one of the most valuable private collections of Egyptian artifacts. But despite his successes, Carter was obsessed with finding the tomb of the mostly unknown boy king Tutankhamun. Years passed with no results and

Egyptologist Howard Carter in 1924

Carnarvon, whose money was funding Carter's quest, was running out of patience. He often wondered what Carter could have uncovered if only he hadn't been distracted by the promise of Tutankhamun. After over a decade, Carnarvon issued Carter an ultimatum. Carter had one more year to find Tutankhamun's tomb; if he failed, he would no longer receive funding of any sort.

Finally, on November 4, 1922, under debris from the tomb of Rameses IV, Carter uncovered a staircase that led to a doorway. Inscribed upon the door was the name Tutankhamun. On November 26, Carter reached the plaster blocks of the tomb and late in the afternoon, he broke through.

With a candle in hand, Carter peered into the darkness that lay just beyond the fissure he had opened. At first, he saw little, but then his eyes adjusted to the darkness and the room and its riches came into view. Carnarvon, who was standing anxiously and unable to bear the silence any longer, asked Carter, "Can you see anything?"

Carter could only bring himself to say, "Yes, wonderful things."

For over 3300 years, the tomb of Tutankhamun had lain undisturbed. By Carter's estimation, the grave robbers had spirited away some of Tutankhamun's wealth, but almost all of it was still intact. The royal seal of the door was unbroken; thieves had only been able to penetrate one of the outer walls. Carter got the sense from the excavation that the tomb had been hastily assembled to accommodate the unexpected and early death of Tutankhamun.

Carter's discovery included the gold mask of King Tutankhamun, which has become synonymous with ancient Egypt.

Three of its four chambers were unadorned, but they held priceless artifacts. Carter had broken into the antechamber and found dismantled chariots and gilded containers of food, thrones and couches. Carter wrote in his diary that everywhere there was "the glint of gold." In the treasury, Carter found four gilded statues of Egyptian goddesses, silent sentries placed around the chest in which Tutankhamun's internal organs were kept. Yet these riches paled in comparison to what Carter unearthed in the burial chamber itself.

The only room to contain murals, the burial chamber held a wondrous gilded shrine. Within this work was a stone sarcophagus that held three coffins. The innermost coffin was cast out of solid gold. Here rested the mummified remains of Tutankhamun and the gold mask, with its unblinking eyes and almost arrogant stare, which has become synonymous with ancient Egypt ever since.

Carter had become an overnight celebrity, and the international media intensified the public's already rabid fascination with Egypt. Carter's success was short-lived, as the historical and cultural significance of his discovery was swept away by whispers and rumors of King Tut's Curse and what Carter had awoken in the dark.

The tombs of pharaohs had long been thought of as cursed places. Arabs who had arrived in Egypt in the 7th century found the hieroglyphics adorning many of the tombs' strange and haunting runes. Shocked by the amazingly well preserved bodies of the mummies, they believed that the tombs were enchanted places, capable of giving life back to the dead. In the following centuries, many grave robbers lost their lives in the long and labyrinth-like corridors that were common in the pharaohs' tombs. Their deaths started a minor flurry of speculation, but Carter's discovery set off the storm.

Legend has it that when Carter returned to his home after uncovering Tutankhamun's tomb, he discovered that his pet yellow canary had been killed by a cobra. His servant, familiar with the stories of cursed tombs, grabbed Carter and thrust under his nose a handful of yellow feathers.

Many believe that Carter also uncovered an ancient curse in the boy king's tomb.

"It is a warning, sir," he said in a stern and unwavering voice. "Wadjet, the serpent and protector of the pharaohs, has sent you a warning. Leave the tomb alone, sir. Leave it alone. Great harm will come to you and others if you do not."

Carter dismissed the story with a wave of his hand. The feathers in his servant's outstretched hand drifted away. "Just get rid of the bird, please. And go home. Your talk wearies me. I don't believe in curses, just what I can see, hear, taste and touch."

"You must listen, sir," the servant pleaded. "The people say there is a curse. They say you will not talk about it because then your men will leave. These treasures…they are not meant for you. They are not meant for us. You and the others will only find death, sir."

Carter had heard enough. "I did nothing of the sort." He thundered at his quivering servant. "These are folk-tales! Nothing more. Tales written and told to frighten petty thieves. Now, I thought I told you to leave! I'll not tell you again."

Months passed and various articles of Tutankhamun's tomb were catalogued and carted away, to be displayed eventually in Cairo's Egyptian Museum and the Luxor Museum. Not one unexplained or mysterious event was reported and Carter felt certain that there was indeed no curse. But on April 5, 1923, at the age of 57, Lord Carnarvon died suddenly of pneumonia in Cairo after being bitten by a mosquito on the left cheek.

When Carnarvon expired, Cairo itself was suddenly plunged into total darkness. Thousands of miles away in Berkshire, England, Carnarvon's son reported that the family dog howled in agony and then dropped dead. People decided these events couldn't have been mere coincidences. They found no reasonable cause for the Cairo blackout and assumed that Tutankhamun was angry and was taking his revenge. Like a runaway carriage, the story gained momentum in 1925 when Tutankhamun's mummy was unwrapped, revealing a face that bore a wound exactly where Carnarvon had been bitten by the disease-infested mosquito that had carried him to his death.

Did a blackout in Cairo have something to do with the curse?

By 1929, newspaper accounts had eagerly attributed 11 unnatural deaths to the mummy's curse. Among the reported dead were two of Carnarvon's relatives, Carter's secretary, Richard Bethell and Bethell's father, Lord Westbury. Six years later, the number of dead had climbed to 21. If the media reports were to be believed, there was indeed a curse.

Carter read the stories, but never wavered from his belief that there was no curse and that it had been the creation of a sensationalistic press. Indeed, if there had been a curse, wouldn't Carter, the man who had first entered the tomb, have been among its victims? He spent the years following the discovery of Tutankhamun's tomb in blissful retirement, collecting Egyptian antiquities for himself and living a relatively quiet and peaceful life at Luxor's Old Winter Palace Hotel. In 1939, the 65-year-old Carter returned to his birthplace of Kensington. He died on March 2, and curse detractors are careful to stress that he had died of natural causes.

Noted Egyptologist and director of the Metropolitan Museum of Art in New York City, Herbert E. Winlock, conducted his own study to disprove the curse's validity in the 1930s. According to his calculations, of the 22 people present at the opening of the tomb in 1922, just six had died by 1934. Of the 22 present for the opening of the sarcophagus in 1924, a mere two had died. Of the ten who had watched the unwrapping of Tutankhamun's mummy, every one was still alive in 1934. The curse was proving remarkably slow to act on its promise to bring swift death to those who trespassed.

Despite the contradictory evidence, people still believe in King Tutankhamun's curse. After all, it is a fascinating and grim story that speaks to our darkest and deepest fears concerning death and the afterlife. Its appeal is timeless and universal, and regardless of whether people believe in the mummy's curse, it has been a boon to Egyptologists and the country itself.

The Cemeteries of Athens

ATHENS, OHIO

Athens, Ohio, has been ranked by the British Society for Physical Research as one of the most haunted places on earth, and it certainly appears to be an area in harmony with the activities of the seemingly undead. In addition to strange stories of spiritualists and witches, the city's cemeteries are the subject of numerous accounts for which there are no logical or rational explanations.

One of the more popular accounts centers on the death of an Ohio University student, David Tischman, in April 1970. In Hanning Cemetery, located in Peach Ridge, a séance was held in an attempt to contact his spirit. Equipment used included a Ouija board and two black candles. The indicator on the board didn't move once but wax from the candles dripped onto the board and pooled into the shape of letters. It read DAVT4. To those conducting the seance, David Tischman had indeed made contact, but what did the 4 represent? It didn't take long to make the connection that Tischman had died in April, the fourth month of the year. Simms Cemetery, another one in Peach Ridge, is believed to be haunted because John Simms had been the official in charge of hanging criminals. It's believed his victims are still out there, attempting to exact revenge for what they perceive to be unjust deaths. Simms himself apparently still wanders the ground, coming out at twilight decked out in a hooded robe.

Other cemeteries in Athens are venues for the strange and unusual. On West State Street, there is a statue "Dedicated to the sacred memory of the unknown dead who rest here 1806–1924." The West State Cemetery is one of the oldest in Athens, and the statue, carved in the shape of an angel, watches over those buried in unmarked graves. Her silent vigil invokes the memory of soldiers who sacrificed their lives in defense of their beliefs, their culture and their customs. Known as the "crying angel," the stone angel will, on occasion, flutter her wings, as both students and residents of Athens have reported. Peer into her face and you might observe tears trickling down her cheeks as the angel weeps for the fallen. Some claim that the angel was built as a memorial to a child who died much too young, and that the statue weeps on the child's birthday.

Bethel Cemetery also has its share of mystery. A group of a dozen graves has heads facing north, a departure from normal custom in which the graves face east so that the dead face the rising sun. Naturally, it is curious that just a dozen in this cemetery break from tradition. Folklorists and researchers offer the explanation that these people were perhaps once witches (practitioners of black and white magic), a hypothesis based on the belief that the witch heaven of Summerland lies towards the north.

These graves are not the only markers of the occult in Athens. When interconnected on a map of the city, the five cemeteries form a path in the shape of a pentagram. The pentagram has long been associated with evil of all sorts, but the symbol has, since ancient times, been one of

Cemeteries in Athens, Ohio, are charged with paranormal energy.

great significance for the followers of God. The Hebrews saw the five-pointed star as a symbol of truth, with its five points representing the books of the Pentateuch. The city of Jerusalem employed the symbol as its seal. Early Christians also adopted the sign, using its five points as a reminder of the five wounds of Christ. In ancient Greece, the followers of Pythagoras saw the pentagram as the pent-alpha, formed by five A's and incorporating the golden ratio. Medieval worshippers saw the pentagram as an "endless knot" that stood for truth and protection against demons. It was worn as an amulet, both for the person and the home. Even witches, who are often associated with evil intentions, view the pentagram as a symbol of noble empowerment, able to provide both knowledge and protection. Its five points represent the elements: spirit, water, fire, earth and air.

The pentagram formed by the cemeteries in Athens has been said to create a safety zone against evil, protecting the city and its people from forces that might threaten their safety. The zone supports the views of the spiritualists who believed that Athens was a highly spiritual place, an area where courageous, able and strong individuals were able to contact the mystics and have the past, present and future revealed to them. As a result, some believe that when chaos strikes in the form of earthquakes, fires and floods that destroy the monuments of man, Athens will remain untouched. The spirit world, however, can intervene in the lives of those who might stumble upon misfortune.

Take, for example, the story of an Ohio University student. For nights on end, he experienced the same dream involving a Lady in White who warned against accepting a friend's offer of a ride on a motorcycle. Days later, he suddenly realized why he'd been visited by this persistent vision. A friend of his did in fact ride up to his home one day to ask if he would like to accompany him on a motorcycle ride through the country. Remembering the Lady in White, the student refused. A short time later, his friend crashed into a tree and died. The student's life had been saved by his recurring dream.

Fox Family Channel named Athens as one of the United States' scariest places in 2000. Needless to say, some of the many accounts are legends that have been exaggerated over time, as myths tend to be. Details are changed, gore is amplified, tragedy is multiplied. But regardless of how the stories have evolved over time, the obscuring of the facts does not diminish the firm belief in the powerful presence of the paranormal in Athens.

Hollywood Forever Cemetery

HOLLYWOOD, CALIFORNIA

Given America's obsession with celebrity and stardom, it's a little surprising that people were ready to close up Hollywood Memorial Cemetery permanently just five years ago. The cemetery is the famous resting site for Hollywood luminaries such as director Victor Fleming, who counted among his credits both *The Wizard of Oz* and *Gone with the Wind*, actor and director John Huston, actress Jayne Mansfield and early silent screen idol Rudolph Valentino. Bankrupt and decrepit, the cemetery desperately needed not just a new owner, but also one with particularly deep pockets. Though the asking price for the cemetery was just $375,000, estimates for the cemetery's restoration would add at least $7 million to the bill.

On land that was once part of the Grower family's wheat fields, the Hollywood Memorial Cemetery was founded in 1899 with 100 acres at its disposal. It was Hollywood's first cemetery. Forty of those acres were sold to Paramount Studios and RKO Radio Pictures in 1920, and today Paramount's prop house marks the cemetery's southern boundaries. Situated near a number of Hollywood's thriving movie studios, the cemetery quickly became a popular final resting place with studio heads, actors and writers. Even notorious gangsters, such as Ben "Bugsy" Siegel, whose lives were both glamorous and tragic, clamored to be laid to rest at Hollywood Memorial. Its picturesque grounds of palm trees, immaculately groomed lawns and reflecting ponds became the back-drop for a number of stunning mausoleums and statues that were as grand as the men and women they memorial-ized. Silent and still, the air was only broken with the ele-giac pealing of the Eliza Otis Bells that rang out from its perch atop the Santa Monica Boulevard entrance. Sometimes, it was punctured with gasps and exclamations whenever one of its three ghosts are seen or heard by astonished visitors. At Hollywood Memorial Cemetery, even death could be made fashionable. Unfortunately, the same couldn't be said for the cemetery itself.

By the late 1990s, the cemetery was just a pale reflec-tion of its former self. Grass had either overrun the ceme-tery or died, leaving barren yellow patches. Its owner, Jules Roth, who had owned the graveyard since 1940, had done the unthinkable by raiding mausoleums for statues that he would later sell for profit. He had let rain pour in through patchy roofs that had needed repairs, left crypts shattered and cracked from earthquakes and sold por-tions of the cemetery for strip malls to use to cover his debts. Conditions had deteriorated to the point that most of the cemetery's profits extended not from burials, but from disinterments. Not only were people no longer being buried at Hollywood Memorial, but descendants were removing their ancestors to be buried elsewhere. Vagrants wandered into the cemetery from Santa Monica Boulevard and made their home amidst the ruins. But it was not until Roth's death in 1998 that the extent of his treachery was revealed. A fund that had been established long ago to guarantee the cemetery's survival in perpetu-ity was missing close to $9 million. Roth might as well

Hollywood Forever Cemetery in Los Angeles

have had razed the cemetery. Bankrupt, the cemetery had few options.

Tyler Cassity couldn't believe that this great piece of American history might be lost and saw a chance not just to expand his St. Louis-based family's cemetery holdings, but to marry technology with the traditional funeral that is as old as time itself. He has plans to create interactive films that could be accessed from plinths scattered throughout the cemetery. Films with photos and testimonials would recreate the lives of those interred beneath the ground for a more immediate and intimate cemetery experience. Recognizing the power of the Internet, Cassity had plans to equip the funeral chapel to transmit ceremonies live to friends and family unable to attend.

Forever Enterprises, Cassity's company, bought the Hollywood Memorial Cemetery. To mark the occasion, the Hollywood Memorial Cemetery was renamed Hollywood Forever Cemetery and the company embarked on restoring the cemetery's faded luster and attracting the rich and famous to its grounds once again.

The restoration continues and Hollywood Forever Cemetery still has its ghosts who, much like Cassity's vision, resurrect the past whenever they appear. One particular scandal surrounding the death of a young struggling actress, Virginia Rappe, riveted and polarized the Hollywood community of Los Angeles. It will never die so long as she continues to haunt her grave.

To the public, he was Fatty Arbuckle, a portly and jolly man who threw his heavy frame around with surprisingly acrobatic abandon to the gleeful laughter of rapt audiences. To his friends, he was Roscoe Arbuckle, who was a fastidious and sensitive soul. But when struggling actress Virginia Rappe was pronounced dead on September 9, 1921, just days after partying with Arbuckle and his friends at the St. Francis Hotel in San Francisco, Arbuckle was thrust into a role that he never wished to play.

Once seen as a gifted comedian with the skills to rival comic legends such as Charlie Chaplin and Buster Keaton, Arbuckle was now cast as the villain upon the Hollywood stage, accused of raping Virginia Rappe, which contributed to her death from peritonitis. Newspapers vilified Arbuckle, and while the public once embraced his jolly persona, they now saw him as a monster who lived a life of excess and debauchery. It was the first in a long and notorious line of Hollywood scandals led by newspaper magnate William Randolph Hearst. Sensationalism, not truth, won out in the court of public opinion.

Virginia Rappe, nee Rapp (Rappe added the "e" later in life, claiming that it was more elegant), had lived in New York and Chicago before she headed west where her striking good looks won her work as a model and an actress. As a teenager, Rappe had been known for her promiscuous ways and was believed to have had several abortions before her 16th birthday. In San Francisco, she caught the eye of director Henry Lehrman and the two began a tempestuous relationship that lasted four years. In 1921, the couple split for good.

That year, Arbuckle's career had never looked better. He was under contract to Paramount and was making $1 million a year, a princely sum in those days. Movies like *Brewster's Millions* and *Gasoline Gus* had audiences in stitches and Arbuckle was working prodigiously, making close to six films a year. The workload was hectic, however, and Arbuckle was beginning to waver under the stress. He drank more and became moody and defensive when inebriated. A director friend, Fred Fischbach, decided that the best thing for Arbuckle would be a three-day vacation to

Before the scandal, Fatty Arbuckle was one of the most popular comedic actors of Hollywood's pre-sound era.

San Francisco. Eager for a break, Arbuckle agreed and, along with actor Lowell Sherman, Arbuckle and Fischbach drove to the city. Once there, they rented three adjoining rooms at the St. Francis Hotel. On September 5, 1921, the fates of Fatty Arbuckle and Virginia Rappe would be forever entwined.

No one knows whose idea it was to throw a party at the St. Francis, but it was a raucous affair, fueled with outlawed liquor. Inhibitions were dropped and passions rose. No one knows who invited Virginia Rappe, but the young actress arrived with her manager, Al Semnacher, and a woman, "Bambina" Maude Delmont, in tow. Arbuckle was not pleased. Delmont was a notorious woman who spent almost as much time at the police station as she did out of it, constantly brought up on charges of extortion, bigamy and fraud. Her job, at times, was to lure husbands into trysts, which were photographed and used for blackmail or extortion. In the case against Arbuckle, Delmont would become the comedian's most vocal accuser.

In the early hours of the morning, Arbuckle stumbled into his bathroom, only to find Rappe sprawled along the floor. He carried her out to a bed, at which point Rappe asked for water. Arbuckle obliged her and then left the room, thinking that she had just a few too many drinks.

But when Arbuckle returned to the bedroom, he found Rappe rolling on the floor, moaning and groaning in pain. He picked her up again and placed her on the bed. Delmont chose that moment to walk into the room when Rappe began screaming and grabbing at her clothing. The hysteria drew a crowd of partygoers who watched with surprise as Rappe yelled at Arbuckle to stay away from her.

Looking at Delmont, Rappe said, "What did he do to me, Maudie? Roscoe did this to me."

While the party picked up again as if it hadn't even missed a beat, physicians were called in to examine Rappe, and they all concluded that the woman was merely drunk. The hotel physician took pity upon the young woman's distress and gave her a dose of morphine. Rappe was still in some pain and her friend Delmont believed that she knew why.

Quietly and quickly, she told the doctor that Rappe had only fallen ill after Arbuckle had dragged her into his hotel bedroom and raped her. She ignored the fact that doctors were unable to find any physical evidence on Rappe's body to support her allegations.

Rappe was admitted to a hospital with a blisteringly high fever, but it was too late. She died on September 9. An autopsy revealed the cause of death to be peritonitis, an inflammation and infection of the abdominal lining. The infection was traced back to a ruptured bladder. But what had caused her bladder to rupture? Most people believed that Fatty Arbuckle was the culprit.

Arbuckle was arrested for first-degree murder, though the charge would be later dropped to manslaughter. Authorities alleged that when Arbuckle raped Rappe, the violent act tore her bladder, directly leading to the condition that would kill her. The case went to trial three times.

In the first trial, the prosecution's case fell apart when key witnesses claimed that they had been forced to sign statements under duress. Most suspicious of all to observers was that the woman who had landed Arbuckle in this predicament, "Bambina" Maude Delmont, never testified. Arbuckle took the stand and his testimony, which never wavered under a thundering cross-examination, did little to reverse public opinion about the disgraced comedian. The most damning of all, at least for the prosecution, was that the tear in Rappe's bladder had not been caused by any sort of external force. The defense was certain that they would be victorious, but unfortunately the jury could not reach a decision. Of the 12 jurors, ten were in favor of acquittal. The other two could not be convinced that Arbuckle was innocent.

The second trial led to another deadlocked jury. Ten voted for conviction, while two opted for acquittal. In the third and final trial, there was no doubt among the jurors. Arbuckle had been wrongly accused and after a very brief deliberation, the jury was unanimous in their support for acquittal. Arbuckle's nightmare was over.

No one knows how Rappe's bladder was ruptured, but there are a number of theories, all of which played upon her promiscuous past. One claimed that Rappe had a botched, illegal abortion that led to a ruptured bladder. Venereal diseases could have also explained the peritonitis. Others pointed out that cirrhosis of the liver may have led to peritonitis, since Rappe was a heavy drinker. Arbuckle, it seemed, had had the misfortune of being in the wrong place at the wrong time.

Though acquitted and cleared of any involvement in the actress' death, Arbuckle's reputation lost its luster. The three trials had basically bankrupted him and he was painted, rightly or wrongly, as the symbol of Hollywood's excesses. Paramount terminated his contract and his films were pulled from circulation. He certainly couldn't make new ones, as studios did their best to avoid his stigma. Arbuckle retreated behind the camera where he directed a number of films under the name William B. Goodrich. The work, however, was far from satisfying.

By the early 1930s, it appeared that Arbuckle was on his way back to respectability. He had found work in front of the camera and Warner Brothers soon offered him a contract. But at 46, Arbuckle's heart had grown weak and he died in his sleep. The cause was heart disease, but long-time friend Buster Keaton would always say that Fatty Arbuckle had "died of a broken heart."

As for Virginia Rappe, she was buried at Hollywood Memorial Cemetery, where her spirit continues to lurk.

When Steve Landon (an alias) came to Hollywood Memorial Cemetery in the late 1980s, it was because he had always loved Hollywood, or at least Hollywood in its earliest and original incarnation. He loved films like *Gone with the Wind*, actors like Douglas Fairbanks and directors like Cecil B. Demille.

"They told stories, you know," Landon says from his home in Tempe, Arizona. "They weren't films born out of market research and demographics. People had great stories that they wanted to tell and to share and they did."

Naturally, when Landon went west to California to visit his sister, a stop at the Hollywood Memorial Cemetery was a must.

"She didn't really want to go, but hey, she's a great sister and she did," Landon says, "In the end, of course, she was thrilled that she had. She never would have heard the sobbing."

Landon brought along not just his camera, but also a videotape recorder, ready to document every step through the cemetery on his tour. His sister followed patiently behind, watching with a mixture of amusement and trepidation as his brother darted eagerly from one monument to the next. He had a list of names and it didn't take long for him to work his way through most of the alphabet. He'd started with Princess Sylvia Ashley, late wife of both

Douglas Fairbanks and Clark Gable, then to actors Peter Finch and Peter Lorre.

Landon's tour had taken most of the morning and a large part of the afternoon. His sister was a little tired, but she soldiered on. As the sun began to sink towards the horizon and shadows began to lengthen, Landon began to look for Virginia Rappe's grave. He found it, nestled among the grass and flowers. It was a simple headstone, bare and plain. There was her name, and beneath it, the years 1895–1921 and nothing more. She had died at such a young age, just 26 years old.

Landon snapped a couple of photographs while recounting Rappe's life story to his sister. He had just placed a check next to her name when he heard it.

"It was the strangest thing," Landon says. "My sister and I were walking away to find another grave and I remember how quiet everything suddenly seemed. I could still hear the traffic from Santa Monica Bouvelard, but there was a real stillness to everything. And yeah, the sun was setting, but suddenly, I just felt a chill. My sister felt it too. And then we heard the most bizarre thing. It was a sobbing, a real choking, deep in the throat sort of sobbing. I remember looking into my sister's eyes and without saying a word, I knew that she was hearing it too. We didn't think it was all too strange. We were in a cemetery after all, and people cry in cemeteries."

The two siblings stopped and turned to find the source of the sobbing. They looked around but only saw visitors like themselves walking with a reverential awe around the cemetery. No one seemed particularly distressed or unhappy.

One cemetery visitor had a paranormal encounter near Virginia Rappe's gravestone.

"Only then," recalls Landon, "did we understand that the sobbing was coming not from around us, but beneath our feet. It was a bit of an epiphany, absolutely mind-blowing. We'd never really thought too much about ghosts, but I mean, really, if it's coming from the ground...what else then could it be?"

Landon and his sister walked ever slowly back from where they had come, as if haste might silence the cries. The sobbing grew louder as they approached Rappe's grave; standing there, Landon realized the unmistakable truth.

"No doubt about it," he says, his voice rising with excitement, "it was coming from her grave. We couldn't believe it. It was absolutely incredible. It was coming through the ground and the headstone clear as a bell. I remember my sister even getting down on her hands and knees and pressing her ear to the ground. She stood back up and just stared and stared at the ground. She was absolutely fascinated. And of course, so was I.

Landon had heard that Hollywood Memorial Cemetery was haunted, but he never really gave much thought to it. After all, it seemed that most cemeteries were haunted but few people had ever actually seen or heard a ghost.

"Everyone knows someone who knows someone who's seen something. But you never hear about it directly. But yeah," Landon admits, "I was wrong. Grossly mistaken, as it turns out, because it happened to me."

Asked to hazard a guess as to why Rappe's spirit might be sobbing, Landon, who admits that his guess would be nothing more than just speculation, answers that perhaps Rappe continues to weep because of her aborted life.

"Maybe she's also crying because she realizes that her past caught up with her. Or maybe she cries because she just wants to be loved—she grew up in a home without a father and a mother who died when she was just eleven," Landon elaborates. "I know it's cliché, the broken home explanation and all, but it had to have had an effect."

Landon encountered just one of the three legendary ghosts that reside at Hollywood Forever Cemetery. Two others have long captivated the imaginations and roused the curiosities of both those who recall Hollywood's earliest days fondly and those who devote their lives to seeking out the paranormal. Ghost hunters have come often to Hollywood Forever to uncover the truth behind its hauntings and have had success in encountering both the Lady in Black and Clifton Webb, even though both have been dead for decades.

In life, the Lady in Black was known as Ditra Flame and she would have been the envy of almost every red-blooded woman in the United States. After all, one of her mother's closest friends was none other than Rudolph Valentino, one of America's first sex symbols and arguably its most iconic, with a star wattage rivaling and even surpassing that of Marilyn Monroe's and James Dean's. As it was with Monroe and Dean, Valentino's early death only added to his mystique and his legend. In death, he attained immortality and remained forever young with his dashing good looks, piercing gaze and wry smile undimmed and untouched by time and age.

Valentino and Flame were friends from the time that Flame was very young. As a child, Flame was sickly and spent many days and weeks trapped within the dreary confines of a hospital. Her mother, devastated as any mother would be, beseeched her friend Valentino to visit the poor child. Graciously, Valentino did, always bringing with him a single red rose that did much to dispel Flame's anxiety. After giving Flame the flower, Valentino would then sit beside her on her bed, hold her hand and speak to her. Flame would listen raptly, finding comfort in the mingled scents of the cologne he wore and the tobacco he smoked. It was a kindness that Flame never forgot, and she remembered forever the promise that she had made to the actor.

One time, Valentino had said to Flame, "If I die before you do, please come and stay by me. I don't want to be alone either. You come and talk to me." Flame promised that she would. She did not expect that she would have to fulfill that promise just a few years later.

Valentino had immigrated to the United States from Italy as a young man, ambitious and eager. He worked briefly as a gardener's assistant on Long Island but soon found work as a dancer in New York City. On tour with a show called *The Masked Model*, Valentino caught the attention of casting agents in California. Though he was usually cast as a minor villain in his early films, those who watched him could not deny his charisma and his talents. He oozed sensuality and when he was cast in the leading role in *The Four Horsemen of the Apocalypse*, audiences embraced his portrayal of Julio, which was infused with that rare combination of bold sexuality and touching sensitivity. 1921's *The Sheik* is the film with which Valentino is most associated. It is that film that conferred upon him the title of "The Great Lover," and his performance had women fainting in the aisles of film houses. But the pressures of stardom broke Valentino. A failed marriage to his great love, Natacha Rambova, and the stresses of promoting *The Son of the Sheik* had taken their toll. Backlash against his escalating stardom was epitomized in the

One of the cemetery's elegant mausoleums

pages of *The Chicago Tribune*, which proclaimed that Valentino was little more than a "painted pansy." He suffered from terrible ulcers, which he exacerbated with long nights drinking away his sorrows in speakeasies. He had arrived in New York for the premiere of his film, but on

August 15, Valentino collapsed in his hotel room at the Ambassador. Eight days later, at the age of 31, Rudolph Valentino was dead. The cause was peritonitis, the same condition that had claimed Rappe's life. An ulcer had become perforated in his abdominal cavity and infection had followed. From all accounts, his anguished and tortured last moments had the actor writhing and moaning in pain until death itself became a sweet relief. An estimated 100,000 people turned out for his funeral services in New York City. Thousands more greeted his body as it was carried by train to Los Angeles. He was laid to rest in Hollywood Memorial in Cathedral Mausoleum as mourners watched and a plane showered thousands of rose petals upon the ground below.

Along with hundreds of thousands of women and men who had come to admire Valentino's work and untapped potential, Ditra Flame was devastated and heartbroken. She remembered the promise that she had made and swore that she would not break her word. Starting in 1926, Flame went to Hollywood Memorial, dressed all in black, bearing with her all her grief and a bouquet of blood-red roses that she placed before Valentino's tomb. For years, Flame returned on the anniversary of Valentino's death to honor and preserve his memory, dressed always in that black dress that contrasted sharply with the roses that she held against her chest.

Her annual visits attracted the attention of the media, who dubbed Valentino's faithful mourner the Lady in Black. Not surprisingly, many women had their own stories to tell about Valentino and many of them purported to be the original Lady in Black. The coverage and speculation proved increasingly grating to Flame and in 1947, at the end of her patience, she finally stepped forward and broke her silence to reveal her story. She hoped that now that the Lady in Black had been unmasked, she could make her trips free of scrutiny. Flame was mistaken.

In 1954, when escalating media attention surrounding the Lady in Black had reduced what had been her simple memorial into a national spectacle, Flame made her last visit to Valentino's tomb. She would not return again until 1977, having discarded her black garb but not the red roses. Flame died in 1984, and her tombstone in San Jacinto, California, proclaims for all to read: "Lady in Black." But so firmly did she hold to her promise to Valentino that not even death keeps her from making her visits. Though other living and breathing Ladies in Black continue Flame's work, the original will not be denied. Her spirit is still seen kneeling before Valentino's tomb. When she leaves, witnesses cannot fail to see that the vases that hang from his tomb have been filled with roses.

Joan Miron knows that the stories about Flame's ghost are often cast aside as little more than rumor or speculation. But Joan knows them to be true. "I didn't see the Lady in Black," Joan is careful to point out, "but I know she was there."

Joan remembers the day clearly. It was cool, at least by Los Angeles standards, and some rain was falling. She was supposed to meet a friend for lunch, but her friend had canceled at the last minute. Joan had already driven from her suburban home in the San Fernando Valley when her friend called; she had little wish to get back onto the freeways of Los Angeles so quickly. Instead, she decided to spend her afternoon walking the streets of Hollywood and, on impulse, decided to stop in at the Hollywood Forever Cemetery.

"I'd never been there before," she says, "but I knew that tons of stars were buried there. For a housewife from Iowa, it was the closest I was going to get to a Hollywood party."

Joan entered the cemetery and made her way to the Cathedral Mausoleum. She wanted to see the final resting place of Rudolph Valentino. Her heels clicked loudly upon the marble floor, echoing through its long wide halls.

"The place was deserted. It was just me and the dead," Joan recalls. "But for some reason, I couldn't shake this feeling that I was being watched."

Joan walked down a hallway on her left and there, found Valentino. She stood for a moment in silence, wondering which famous men and women might have trod the same ground upon which she now stood. She couldn't help but notice that the two vases that hung on either side of the plaque bearing Valentino's name sat empty. It was a miserable sight, she remembered thinking. She ran her hand across the raised letters of his name, and they felt cool to her touch. Sighing, Joan turned and began making her way back to the mausoleum's entrance.

"That's when I saw something out of the corner of my eye," she says. "I don't know what it was. It was like a shadow and it disappeared as soon as I looked directly at it." Slightly spooked, Joan paused and listened for footsteps. She heard nothing, but her own breath had suddenly grown haggard and raspy.

"I was a little scared," she says.

After standing still in the halls of the mausoleum for what seemed like an eternity, Joan began walking to the mausoleum's only entrance and exit. And then she saw the shadow again.

"Something brushed past me," she says. "I'm positive. I felt something push past me on my arm, but when I looked, there was nobody there."

Spurred on by a curiosity that had overtaken her fear, Joan turned back and began walking down the hallway to Valentino's tomb once again. Why she did, she does not know. Her heels clicked upon the marble floor once again and as she neared Valentino's tomb, she couldn't help but notice that the vases, empty mere moments ago, were now holding long-stemmed red roses.

"My jaw dropped," Joan says. "No one was in that mausoleum except me. I'm certain that no one came in or out of that building while I was in there. Except, of course, for that strange shadow." Joan remembers reaching and touching, ever so gently, one of the roses' petals. It felt real. The roses weren't just some sort of mirage or hallucination. Joan just couldn't believe what she had seen. She was convinced that the shadow had something to do with the flowers.

When she returned home later that afternoon, she began doing research on her computer and found dozens of websites describing with great detail the phantom mourner of Rudolph Valentino's tomb. It didn't take her long to find the name Ditra Flame.

"It had to be her that left those flowers," Joan says, her voice firm with conviction. "Who else could it have been? Even if I didn't see someone in the mausoleum, I definitely would have heard someone. It echoes in there. It had to be Ditra Flame's ghost."

No spectral woman pays homage to Clifton Webb. Instead, it's his very own spirit that returns from time to time to haunt his tomb.

Webb, born in Indianapolis, Indiana, in 1889, came to Los Angeles in the early 1920s after stints singing with the Boston Opera Company and dancing in the music halls and nightclubs of New York City. He was something of a prodigy and was already an experienced actor, singer and dancer by the time he was a teenager. Appearances on the stages of both Broadway and London garnered him positive reviews and Hollywood took notice.

His big-screen debut came in 1924 with a minor role in *Polly with a Past*. The part won him roles in a succession of other films, but in 1930 Webb returned to Broadway until 1944, when he wowed critics with his deft portrayal of Waldo Lydecker in the film *Laura*. He continued to win recognition for his work in *The Razor's Edge* in 1946 and *Sitting Pretty* in 1948. In the latter film, Webb originated the role with which he would become most associated: the tidy, sarcastic, fussy nanny and housekeeper Mr. Belvedere. The character's popularity led to a succession of sequels but also led to Webb's typecasting as an effeminate snob. Indeed, he had created Mr. Belvedere with such ease that many insisted on not drawing a distinction between the actor and the role.

Like Mr. Belvedere, Webb was a bachelor. He lived with his mother until her death in 1959. She was his constant companion, accompanying him to parties and dances as

Troubled times have come to the cemetery, but some of its grandeur remains intact.

Webb worked his way through the Hollywood circuit. When his mother died, playwright Noel Coward was reported to have said of Webb, "It must be tough to be orphaned at 71."

Webb continued to appear in films throughout the '50s and early '60s, never straying too far from the effete snobs he portrayed so well. It's been said that Clifton Webb was the inspiration for Mr. Peabody, the witty and cultured dog, who traveled through time with his Waybac machine and his pet boy, Sherman, in the Jay Ward cartoon, *Peabody's Improbable History*. In the 1980s, Mr. Belvedere was even resurrected in a television sitcom of the same name with Christopher Hewitt playing the titular character for a modestly successful five years. Webb himself died in 1966 of a heart attack having left an indelible imprint upon American pop culture.

Before he died, Webb swore that he would never leave his home on Rexford Drive in Beverly Hills, even in death. And it seemed that Webb was true to his word, for his apparition was spotted often at the house until it was torn down. Ever since, his spirit is seen exclusively at the Hollywood Forever Cemetery, where he haunts Crypt 2350.

There have been numerous descriptions of his spirit. Some claimed that his apparition appears as a shimmering light, illuminating the hall of the Abbey of the Psalms Mausoleum in which he's interred. Others claimed that he appears as just a regular specter, not glowing, but translucent and clad in the trim dark suits that he seemed to have favored in life. He was especially fond of walking up and down the hall in front of his tomb.

In 1999, the *Columbus Dispatch* published an article by Mike Harden that dealt with the ghosts of Hollywood. In the article, Harden interviewed Duncan St. James, a part-time actor, now deceased, who operated Oh Heavenly Tours. It was a somewhat macabre operation, right down to the hearse from which St. James conducted his tours to the subject matter itself. St. James was interested not just in celebrities, but also in pointing out where they died. Stops in his tour included the Viper Room, where River Phoenix notoriously died of a drug overdose, and the street corner where *I Love Lucy*'s William Frawley dropped dead. One of the stops along his tour was, of course, Hollywood Forever Cemetery. Inside, St. James described to Harden how Webb's ghost has appeared to countless witnesses and how maintenance workers have often been startled when Webb yells after them, "Hey! Come back here!"

Though Oh Heavenly Tours ultimately failed, Webb's tomb at Hollywood Forever Cemetery continues to be a popular site for ghost hunters and movie buffs. Visitors can catch a glimpse of the old and regal Hollywood. It is one of Hollywood's most storied and venerable sites. In a city like Los Angeles, where even a street corner and shop front have their stories to tell, that is no small feat.

Burkholder Cemetery

HAMILTON, ONTARIO

It wasn't exactly haunted, but then again, for those living around Burkholder Cemetery in Hamilton, Ontario, during the early 19th century, life wasn't exactly normal. Most of us recognize that we will eventually die, but prefer to remain ignorant as to when or how we might pass on. People living near Burkholder Cemetery were watchful for the ominous omen that meant that death, in some shape or form, was on its way.

As early as the dawn of the 19th century, people living in and around Mount Hamilton were burying their dead in a plot of land that would become Burkholder Cemetery in 1839. The Burkholder family had first arrived in the area in 1794 when Jacob Burkholder and his wife, Sophia de Roche, were among the first settlers. The cemetery become an official burial ground when David Burkholder granted a deed to a board of trustees. The deed gave to the board a quarter of an acre on which a school and a public burial ground would be built.

In 1850, a church was erected upon the same site. It was a squat one-story building with whitewashed boards covering its exterior. It was a simple and humble place of worship where the people of Mount Hamilton gave voice to their fears and concerns. Though science and reason had long ago supplanted myth and folklore, it did not mean that superstition had gone the way of the dodo. People still placed great value and importance upon the omens and signs that would eventually be casually dismissed as old wives' tales. The story of Burkholder Cemetery, however, is no old wives' tale. Strange things did transpire. The cemetery itself, with its legible but faded tombstones and its stands of trees towering over the site, appeared untouched by the passage of time.

One evening—the year has been lost in the fog of the past but most place the event as taking place during the mid-19th century—the inhabitants of Mount Hamilton noticed something bizarre. Atop the little white church, as the house of worship had been dubbed, many individuals saw what they could only describe as a ball of light running along the ridge of the church roof. With their fingers pointed to the orb as if the act made the impossible possible, an awed crowd watched as the orb moved left and right, then left again, running back and forth along the church roof. It then took flight, soaring above the confused locals.

The orb soared through the night air like an oversized firefly. But suddenly it stopped, hovering over the house of a prominent local, and then it disappeared. It wasn't long before the silence of the night was broken with shouts and exclamations. "Did you see that?" people asked each other. "What was it?" was the inevitable follow-up. And then the conjecture began. Some claimed that it was marked the presence of an angel. Others pointed their fingers at the dead of Burkholder Cemetery, claiming that it was a ghost.

Their voices fell silent though as a high-pitched wail escaped from the house of the prominent local. The crowd looked at one another and raced to the home. They were greeted by a heartbroken and grieving wife whose husband had died just moments before. Though he had been quite ill, she had assumed he was on his way to recovery. That night, however, he had lapsed into a deep sleep, awaking only moments before his death to look into his wife's eyes with a lucidity that had been missing for days. He then quietly expired. The crowd let out an audible gasp as soon as the sobbing wife had finished relating her tale. Could the orb have been the spectral embodiment of death?

For days after, men, women and children alike peered out their windows at night, trying to see the top of the little white church, praying that they would not catch a glimpse of the mysterious orb that portended death for those it stopped over. It seemed as if they had good cause to worry. It wasn't long before the orb reappeared. It took off from its perch above the church and settled atop of another house. Days later, another Mount Hamilton resident was laid to rest in Burkholder Cemetery. The people were very frightened now indeed. At first, people were able to convince themselves that the orb only settled atop the homes of those who had been ill for weeks, even months, but it soon became clear that the orb did not discriminate and settled upon the homes of anyone. Death, it seemed, was lurking around every corner.

Over time, the orb lost its capacity to terrorize. The people began to understand that it wasn't the orb that caused death; instead, the orb was simply a messenger or an omen. Its appearance still devastated households, for the death of a loved one is never easy to bear. In time, the orb became just another part of the rhythm of daily life

*For a young woman who lived near the cemetery, the proximity
became too much to handle.*

around Burkholder Cemetery. For some, the orb was
something of a comfort. With the knowledge that death
was coming, people were able to steel themselves for its
arrival and to treasure the precious moments that
remained.

No one knows exactly when or why the orb stopped
appearing after a period of time. Elders recognized that

young people were unable to view the orb and they blamed it squarely upon the erosion of their God-fearing ways. The orb was nothing less than an angel, though only visible to those whose religious beliefs were strong and pure.

It has been long since anyone was buried at Burkholder Cemetery; most of the tombstones bear the names of those who passed away in the 19th century. It has also been long since anyone saw the orb race along the ridge of the little white church. But like the cemetery, the legends persist, even if the church did not. It was razed in 1955 and was replaced with the current Burkholder United Church, which was built three years later. Its rooftop remains orb-free. But just because the orb no longer frequents Mount Hamilton doesn't mean that the dead have remained peacefully at rest.

Kaitlyn Jones has lived next to Burkholder Cemetery all her life. Just across from her house sits the cemetery, and though Kaitlyn describes her house as "a plain ordinary house that looks like it was inhabited by the girl next door in a movie," her life has been anything but. Burkholder Cemetery looks tranquil enough during the day when the sun bathes the grounds in the rich glow of its warming rays, but at night it is a different story altogether. Lost in shadow, the cemetery looms like a deep black hole from which spooks and spirits might emerge at any moment. Or so Kaitlyn thought when she would crawl under her covers to sleep.

Many nights, Kaitlyn was restless, but she didn't dare look out her window to the cemetery. Her youthful imagination, already living off of a steady diet of nightmarish

tales about the Bogey Man and Dr. Frankenstein's creature, now had an entirely new terrifying scenario. Only in
the company of her family did it seem that she could be
safe from the evils outside. The family took Kaitlyn's terrors all in stride. After all, she was young and would eventually grow out of it. At least that's what they hoped.
Instead, her terrors intensified. And with good reason.
Kaitlyn no longer needed her imagination to be terrified.
The spirits and voices that she heard in her room were
more than enough. Her parents could be forgiven for
thinking that their young daughter was blessed, or cursed,
with a hyperactive imagination and for refusing to hear
her stories. But the fact of the matter was that Kaitlyn was
having some very strange encounters with the paranormal
spirits of Burkholder Cemetery.

It began one night when Kaitlyn was nine years old.
Kaitlyn, whose memory of the night is understandably
fuzzy, estimates that it might have been around 10 PM.
Kaitlyn was cold in the house and wanted a blanket, but
not just any blanket. She wanted the blanket that was in
her mother's car, so she ambled out of the house and
down the driveway. Kaitlyn opened the door, grabbed the
blanket and stopped dead in her tracks. "I looked
over my shoulder," she writes, "and just saw someone. It
looked like a woman with hair slightly longer than shoulder length in a flowing dress." The figure was crouched in
front of a tombstone just across the street and with a look,
sent little Kaitlyn scurrying back into the house. She didn't
tell her parents about the apparition, knowing all too well
that they didn't believe in ghosts and that they would dismiss it with a wave of their hands. She only confided in

her sister. Just four years older, the sister was, more than likely, just as confused as Kaitlyn.

After seeing the woman in the graveyard, Kaitlyn's life returned to normal for a couple of years. But when she turned 11, Kaitlyn had her first encounter with a spirit she has taken to calling "the Lady in Black."

"I was standing in my living room with my sister," Kaitlyn recalls, "and saw the Lady in Black walk by. She had a long auburn-colored braid and a long black dress. She was nowhere near ugly...she had a very soft appearance and was completely silent." The experience was far from jarring and after that first sighting, Kaitlyn continued to see the Lady in Black on a regular basis.

Kaitlyn's life was fast becoming one of anticipation and dread. What would happen next? It was a question she often asked herself and she never waited too long for an answer. Take, for example, the strange voice that sometimes calls out her name.

The first time it happened, Kaitlyn was just sitting in her room doing her homework. Usually, she works with music, but for some reason she chose not to turn on her radio that day. Kaitlyn was sitting at her desk. The radio sat silent next to her desk, which is why it must have come as quite the shock when she heard something that she can only describe as a "child's voice." Given her past experiences, the voice was both unexpected and expected.

It came out as a whisper, so low that she almost couldn't hear it. But she did hear it and once she had, it was all she could hear. The whisper, which first sounded like nothing more than incoherent mumbling, was very clearly speaking her name. Kaitlyn turned from her homework with a start. She stared at her closet door. It was from behind the closet's white doors that she heard the voice.

Kaitlyn stepped quietly away from her desk and crept towards the closet before throwing open the door. She was disappointed. The closet, save for her clothes and shoes, was empty. She'd expected her sister to be sitting inside, snickering and laughing at how she'd scared her. But she wasn't there. Kaitlyn stared into the closet, wondering what was going on. She closed the door and sat back down at her desk and "continued to work in utter silence." But then, she heard her name called out again and then soft laughter. She was alone. And if she was alone, who in the world was whispering her name?

Kaitlyn didn't wait around to find out. Terrified, she fled her bedroom and ran all the way downstairs to the basement where she found her sister. In a staccato cadence, she told her sister what had happened. As the months passed, Kaitlyn heard the voice two more times. Each time, it was the same voice from the closet whispering to Kaitlyn. Each time, Kaitlyn grew more and more accustomed to the voice and when she last heard it, it didn't even cause her to start. She simply sighed and turned back to the book she had been reading in bed.

She still sees the woman too. If the voice and the woman are related, Kaitlyn does not know. She hasn't decided whether the voice whispering her name is that of a woman or a man. It sounds as though it might belong to someone young, leading Kaitlyn to believe that it might have nothing to do at all with the middle-aged woman dressed in black. Lately, Kaitlyn wonders if something might have happened to the woman. When pressed to explain why, Kaitlyn describes how lately, whenever the woman has appeared for a visit, she is no longer dressed in her long black dress.

"The last time I saw her was this past summer, but she was in a white dress, which I take to be something significant." Unfortunately, Kaitlyn cannot even hazard a guess as to what might be the reason behind the lady's change in fashion.

Now 16 years old, Kaitlyn still lives in the haunted home she has known all her life. She still looks out at the cemetery across the street with trepidation, finding its presence altogether creepy.

"To this day," she says, "I still run past the cemetery because it creates such a tense feeling in me. I always wonder to myself how much actually goes on that I don't know about or don't see." Though she may have been terrified to be living next door to a cemetery at the outset, she now embraces the opportunity.

Pragmatically, she adds, "I now approach things from a new level of understanding. I am the only person in my family that experiences these things…People say that there are few people in life that spirits choose to reveal themselves to and I believe that I am just one of the lucky few."

The Stepp Cemetery

MONROE COUNTY, INDIANA

Near the edge of the Stepp Cemetery, close to a small grave, is a tree stump. From that stump, a darkly dressed specter is said to feverishly guard the final resting place of her loved one, someone taken from her by the hands of another.

Some say lightning struck a tree and from its remains this crude chair was roughly hewn. Others claim a relative cut the tree down to create a spot from which he or she could pause and reflect. Regardless, over time the stump has become known as the "Warlock Seat" or the "Witch's Throne." And all because of the legend of the Lady in Black.

The Stepp Cemetery lies deep within the heart of Indiana's Morgan-Monroe State Forest. Even on the sunniest days of summer, the graveyard is lit for just a short while. The rest of the time the tombstones find themselves shrouded within the shadows of the cathedral-like stands of hardwoods, the light barely rippling through the leaves and branches.

The burial ground, located 15 miles north of Bloomington and 5 miles southeast of Martinsville, is named for Reuben Stepp. Stepp, originally of North Carolina, made his way to Indiana in the late 19th century. Despite the barrenness of the land, he purchased property in the township and settled in to raise corn and pigs with his family of nine.

Life at that time was far from idyllic. Whooping cough, dysentery and influenza were prominent, claiming the lives of children from many households clustered in the area. Perhaps it is the mother of one of these unfortunate youngsters who haunts the Stepp Cemetery. Or maybe it's the widow of a man killed during the Civil War.

The apparition reportedly always wears black, which sharply contrasts with her long flowing locks of brilliant white. She's said to be old, even wizened, but far from ugly. Some accounts paint her as heavyset and wearing a black hat with a chain around her leg.

Why the chain? There is speculation that when the husband of the woman in black was killed during the Civil War, she went careening into madness and ended up in a mental institution. Sadly, her insanity prevented her from ever visiting her spouse's grave. So in death she returned to the site, making up for all those years of lost time, all those years chained within her padded cell, pinned under the watchful eyes of physicians and attendants who cared nothing for her grief or loss.

Or perhaps the Lady in Black is watching over her child. In this version of the legend, a family was riding home from church in their wagon. Hidden in the dense forest was a pack of youths. The kids jumped right into the path of the wagon, scaring the horses. The family screamed, the wagon lurched forward and the motion threw the husband and baby from their seats. Tragically, the two did not survive. The mother buried them in the Stepp Cemetery. And to this day, no grass grows on the baby's grave. Moreover, should anyone leave an item on the barren plot of earth, it will be removed by unseen forces to a place less insulting to the woman who watches over her dead child.

Deep in Indiana's Morgan-Monroe State Forest lies the Stepp Cemetery.

Some believe the Lady in Black is there to prevent accidents and tragedies of the past. Like the one in which her daughter was decapitated when the car she was riding in sped off the winding roads of the Morgan-Monroe State Forest and crashed into a tree.

This story goes that one evening the girl and her boyfriend decided to park in the forest. Later, they had to rush back so the girl would be home in time for her cur-few. They hastened off into the night, desperately trying to get home before midnight. Unfortunately, in their rush they neglected to note how many sharp turns and blind corners dotted the road. The boy lost control of the car and it crashed. The two were buried in the Stepp Cemetery, but the girl's head was never found.

Soon after, the girl's mother died and couples parking in the forest found their privacy unexpectedly and horri-fyingly disturbed by the vision of a gnarled old woman, dressed entirely in black, with the battered and bruised head of a young girl hanging from her neck. The mother, it would seem, had risen from the grave, desperate to warn other children about the dangers of speeding along the forest's winding roads.

The stump itself seems cursed with the taint of crimes past. Legend states that anyone who sits on it during an evening will die within the year. Stories abound about individuals who have sat on it and have felt the ice-cold grip of some being around their necks. Others say they've heard both the unearthly cries of a woman in anguish and the mournful melody of a lullaby breaking the hushed silence of the cemetery.

The Stepp Cemetery continues to be used by relatives of those already interred in the grounds of the Morgan-Monroe State Forest. And, it would seem, by the Lady in Black.

Yorba Cemetery

YORBA LINDA, CALIFORNIA

Many people know Yorba Linda, California, as the birthplace of former American president Richard Nixon. But to those with a vested interest in the paranormal, that fact is secondary. For paranormal enthusiasts, Yorba Linda is prominent because it is home to the Pink Lady. Over the years, the Pink Lady has become something of an institution in Yorba Linda. She arouses curiosity and, most importantly, serves as a link between past and present, tying modern Yorba Linda, a city of close to 70,000 residents, to the time of Don Bernardo Yorba, an ancestor of the Pink Lady.

Don Bernardo Yorba was the third son of Jose Antonio Yorba, who had come with Don Gaspar de Portola in 1769 from Spain. In 1834, Yorba successfully petitioned Mexican Governor Jose Figueroa for 13,000 acres of land that rested on the northern banks of the Santa Ana River. He combined that holding with lands that had been given to his father by the King of Spain in 1810 to create one of the grandest *ranchos* of California's Golden Age.

To commemorate his claim, Yorba named his sprawling estate Rancho Canon de Santa Ana, the Canyon of Saint Anne, mother of the Virgin Mary. Yorba was a deeply religious man, committed to both family and the Roman Catholic Church. In 1858, Yorba ceded to the Bishop of the Catholic Church a little plot of land just west of his adobe ranch house. La Mesita, a small rolling hill, would become Yorba Cemetery, the oldest private cemetery in Orange County. Only the Mission Cemetery in San Juan Capistrano is older. When Yorba died, he was buried at Yorba Cemetery, and his holdings passed onto various family members. Over time, Yorba was joined in the cemetery by members of other pioneer families, such as the Carrillos, the Peraltas and the Castillos.

In 1888, the land just north of the Yorba family holdings was abuzz with activity. It stood in marked contrast with the pastoral idyll that the Yorbas had carved out for themselves. A group of speculators and promoters had arrived to establish Carlton, in the hopes that entrepreneurs from the East would be drawn to the warm climate, abundant of water and a railroad, and would create a thriving industrial metropolis. But, in just nine years, Carlton was deserted. The water had turned brackish and the coveted railroad line never arrived. Had it not been for Carlton's failure, Yorba Linda, which was established in 1909, may never have become Orange County's 25th city.

As for Yorba Cemetery, close to 400 individuals were buried within its gates before its closure in 1939. In the following years, the cemetery fell victim to vandals, who defaced marble headstones and made off with a number of tombstones. Many were never recovered, while some were found strewn about the streets of Anaheim. Teenagers used the Yorba Cemetery as a popular hangout. Once manicured and pristine lawns began to resemble the remnants of a frat house party, strewn with beer cans, bottles and cigarettes. Some people believe that the story of the Pink Lady had been created as a deterrent to keep vandals from trespassing. As it happened, the story may have piqued public interest, so people began flocking to Yorba Cemetery with the hopes of spotting the strange spirit.

In 1967, the Orange County Board of Supervisors had had enough. Yorba Cemetery represented the city's history and the county was not going to allow its past to be erased through neglect and apathy. The Catholic Archdiocese of Los Angeles deeded the cemetery to Orange County and with a team of rangers and volunteers, began restoring the cemetery, a labor of love that continues to this day.

Unlike some ghosts, the Pink Lady keeps her appearances tied to a strict and predictable schedule. Her adherence to this schedule has become something of a phenomenon and tradition of its own in Yorba Linda. On the day that she is to appear, Yorba Cemetery becomes a hub of activity. As the hands of the clock approaches midnight on June 15, the grounds of the cemetery become increasingly crowded, thronged with curious onlookers, both local and national, eager to catch a glimpse of the Pink Lady as she emerges from an oleander bush and moves towards the cemetery's rear. It is the only day of the year on which the Pink Lady has been known to appear.

And she doesn't appear in just any year. For reasons both mysterious and murky, the Pink Lady will only appear near midnight on June 15 during even-numbered years. The rarity of her appearances, just five times within any given decade, has only endeared her to the people of Yorba Linda and paranormal enthusiasts. Of course, just because people have gathered doesn't necessarily mean that the Pink Lady will appear. She does have a schedule, but rare is the time that she actually keeps to it.

Still even when she doesn't appear, odd things do happen at tiny Yorba Cemetery as the clock creeps towards the witching hour on June 15. In 1976, reporter Carol Cling wrote that members of the Psychic Science Investigators experienced a number of strange things the night of June 15. They may not have been fortunate enough to have encountered the Pink Lady, but they were wholly convinced that something paranormal lurked within. As they watched and waited, a member of the team suddenly yelled out, *"Por favor espere; yo voy!"* Translated from Spanish, the team member had said, "Please wait. I'm coming!" Of course, in California, it's not such a surprise to hear Spanish spoken. What was a surprise was that the woman who had uttered those words had no idea what she had just said. Indeed, the team member professed that she had never spoken a word of Spanish before in her life. Some people could be forgiven for thinking that the team member was simply exaggerating and perhaps attempting to enliven the mood. But then, it probably wasn't likely that the team member had some sort of control over electronic devices. The team's walkie-talkies and flashlights stopped working shortly after they arrived, only to work again after they left the cemetery. Most observers were convinced too that the pink clouds that threatened to obscure the moon probably had something to do with both the equipment failure as well as the Pink Lady. It isn't very often, after all, that one sees pink clouds in the night sky.

Four years later, in 1980, the Pink Lady again disappointed enthusiasts. Most people left the cemetery a little deflated, but still very much satisfied. Again, electrical

The resident spirit at Yorba Cemetery is rooted in the community's history.

problems plagued the cemetery. The cemetery was, and is, ringed with a condominium complex that illuminates the area with its streetlights. That night in 1980, one, and only one, of the street lamps began to flicker as midnight approached. Twice it flickered and then dimmed, plunging the rear of the cemetery into darkness. Once the flickering stopped, the lamp began casting a pinkish light. Someone noticed that the street lamp stood right over the oleander bush from which the Pink Lady is believed to appear.

It's interesting to wonder what the Pink Lady must think of the enthusiasm with which people await her arrival. What few witnesses there are claimed that hers is a sad apparition, who often pauses to weep over a grave. Whose grave they cannot be sure. Beyond that, little else can be discerned, and there are many who cannot even agree about her appearance. Some have long held that she has long dark hair and deep dark eyes. She appears dressed in a pink gown, from which her name is derived. Others, like psychic Barbara Garcia, disagree.

Garcia, a professional ESP consultant, has worked as a psychic for years, and during that time has acquired a sterling reputation. She first came to national prominence during the late 1970s, when she became involved in the police investigation of the Hillside Stranglers, two cousins who preyed upon young women, even girls, and who stalked the hillsides of Los Angeles.

Her skills were also used in conjunction with the FBI, Interpol and Scotland Yard in high-profile cases like the Yorkshire Ripper in England and Charles Manson's brutal slaughter of Sharon Tate. She has been thoroughly and extensively tested by the Mobius Society, earning a rating of highly accurate during the process. She continues to work from California, searching for missing persons, giving lectures and working as a technical advisor when Hollywood comes calling. But while Garcia had focused her particular abilities upon criminal investigations, she had never used them to explore the paranormal realm. The Pink Lady was the first ghost that she ever investigated and it produced what she calls "fascinating results." It was the latest chapter in what has certainly been a kind of charmed and cursed life for Barbara Garcia.

Garcia has been a professional psychic for many years, but when she was a child, Garcia found her gifts for intuition and perception completely unsettling and mysterious.

"Coming from my background," she recalls, "it was very traumatic. My family was very religious and they thought it was a bad thing."

Garcia herself didn't even know the extent of abilities she possessed. An introvert as a child, Garcia spent many a solitary afternoon just drawing whatever happened to come into her mind. To an outsider, it might have appeared as if Garcia was blessed with a vast and boundless imagination. Her drawings depicted locales she had never been and people she had never met. It wasn't until she was in her early 20s that Garcia began to comprehend exactly what she was able to do.

"The first experience that I can really remember," she says, "I was taking an art class, just something to do in the summer. I was painting and I put out a huge oil painting within 30 minutes. It was just unbelievable. It immediately got a lot of attention. I was in the newspapers because I had my eyes closed while I painted. I was in an altered state, slipping in and out of consciousness." Her eyes may have been closed, but Garcia was not blind. Within her mind, images flickered and flashed, like light on a screen, and didn't stop until she was finished painting.

The ensuing press coverage caught the notice of one of Garcia's neighbors, who happened to be a member of a psychic society. Suddenly, the neighbor inundated Garcia with visits and was always sure to mention the Psychic Research Center in Carlsbad. Garcia dismissed the attention, still unable to reconcile her conservative religious upbringing with her burgeoning abilities. She remembers thinking that the Psychic Research Center was very evil.

Still, the neighbor persisted. She continued to offer Garcia advice and recommended people with whom she could consult. Garcia's skepticism and reluctance continued until the day that a member of the Psychic Research Center, along with the still patient neighbor, came to visit and to look at her artwork.

John Humphrey looked at Garcia's work and immediately asked her how long she had been a psychic artist. Garcia didn't quite know how to answer him; she had little idea of what or who a psychic artist does or is. Humphrey quickly began to describe the world of a psychic artist—their methodology, their work and their sensitivities. As Garcia listened, she realized that Humphrey was describing her experiences. Suddenly, an entire world that Garcia had only explored from the fringes lay wide open before her. As Garcia came to better understand her skills, she began to see them not as a gift, but as a curse.

"I was still really scared when I went to Carlsbad," Garcia recalls, chuckling lightly at her own naïveté. "It was packed with people." But Humphrey reassured her, telling her to just paint whatever came to her mind. So Garcia did. Each drawing elicited admiration from people in the room, especially when Garcia's sketches depicted their own houses, their own cars and their own pets. But amid the accolades, there was a moment of genuine heartbreaking emotion that gave Garcia a fleeting glimpse of how she could affect the lives of others.

"I'll never forget that moment," she says. "I had a drawn a little poodle dog and there was this lady and when she saw the picture, she got hysterical. It turns out that I'd drawn her little dog that had passed away very recently. I thought, *Ok. There's something to this.*"

A curious newspaper reporter, Kevigne Kalisch, came to Garcia in August 1978 and asked her to draw something, which Garcia did. She drew a picture that appeared to be a plane colliding with another plane. The image frightened both Garcia and the reporter, but both didn't really understand its significance. They felt that perhaps its meaning would become clear over time. Garcia told Kalisch to hold onto the picture because "it held the key to something powerful."

So Kalisch waited and began rehearsing a song that she planned to record and give to her friend, Earl, as a Christmas present. Days later, when she told Garcia about Earl, Garcia said, "Earl is going to fall down and he will never receive your record." Kalisch was terrified, "deeply disturbed" in her own words. Garcia had been extremely accurate with her premonitions. In an article that appeared in *The Hefley Report*, Kalisch writes that Garcia hypothesized that perhaps Earl was on the verge of a nervous breakdown. She could not have known the magnitude of the tragedy behind Garcia's picture.

Garcia felt compelled to act. She did not know what she could do for Earl, but felt certain that she could do something about the plane crash. Unfortunately, all her calls to the airlines were ignored. On September 25, 1978, Garcia, Kalisch and all of San Diego mourned.

"Well, it happened," Garcia says matter of factly. "Nobody took us seriously. The plane crashed and [Kalisch] lost a very, very dear friend. It was sad—I was just beginning to understand this stuff, but nobody listened to me."

Among those "torn bodies and debris" lay the remains of Kalisch's friend Earl. When she learned that he was among the victims, Kalisch looked at Garcia's picture and "it was then clear that indeed this was a drawing of an airplane with the yellow of flames surrounding it, a touch of red symbolizing blood and a smoking tail. I could also see a small wing, perhaps from the Cessna, crashing into the jet."

PSA 182 had been brought down by a Cessna. It seemed impossible, but the Boeing 727 and Cessna had collided in mid-air in broad daylight. The Cessna, piloted by a student and his instructor, tore through the 727's right wing, punctured the fuel tank and effectively crippled the plane. A mere 17 seconds later, PSA 182 crashed. It was the first accident for Pacific Southwest Airlines in its 29-year existence and was, at that time, the worst aviation accident in American history.

Kalisch writes, "I experienced terrible shock and grief...I wished that Barbara had better prepared me. But how can someone prepare you to lose one of your best friends?"

The experience left Garcia drained and feeling much as she had after her mother's death, a passing that Garcia claims to have seen before it happened. Garcia was blessed with foresight but unable to affect change. It must be a terrible thing to know the future but remain wholly unable to alter its course. The event demoralized Garcia and, coupled with her recent divorce, led to her "just giving up on life."

Depressed, confused and feeling helpless, Garcia packed a few belongings into her car and ended up in the California wilderness, somewhere just below the La Jolla River Basin. She'd told the few friends she had that she was leaving. For weeks, she lived out of her car until it was towed away.

"I was like a crazy lady," Garcia remembers with a disarming candidness. "For about a year, I lived by this creek." Her days were spent lost in thought, constantly contemplating and questioning her upbringing and her abilities. For sustenance, she watched the deer and beavers, now her only companions, to see what they ate— leaves, berries, weeds and grasses. These were the staples of the animals' diets; they became hers as well.

"It's not a glamorous picture," Garcia says, "but that was my youth." It was a terrible time and could certainly have broken the spirit of many others, but for Garcia it was just the beginning. Fortunately for her, she was squatting on land that belonged to a native reservation. To help supplement its income, the tribe ran a campground near Garcia. Its members had long ago noticed Garcia, occasionally bringing her food but they never called the police. One day, she was told that the campgrounds had been rented out to a group of Hells Angels, passing through en route to a funeral. Garcia was warned to stay away. Curiosity, though, got the better of her.

She sneaked over to the campsite and was caught, spying and eavesdropping. Garcia was terrified. She knew well the reputation of the Hells Angels and frantically wondered what they might do to her. But with a kindness and sympathy that she did not expect, and which Garcia credits for saving her life, the Hells Angels, particularly one called Red and his girlfriend, listened to her story.

"I'm eternally grateful to them," Garcia says graciously. "I talked to them about everything...the trauma, the experience itself. They gave me the time to listen and to allow me to heal. They brought me back into civilization."

She speaks confidently and humorously about it all, fully aware of its role in shaping her character and personality. Self-assured, she seems to have little time for skepticism and doubt, having dealt with both for years as a youth. Embracing her skills, Garcia returned to society and began to use her abilities as best she could.

There is a long history of police departments consulting with psychics in their most difficult and challenging of cases. Garcia believed that she could help with her ESP ability. She no longer doubted herself. Psychic organizations, such as SRI and Mobius, performed all sorts of tests on her, some of which involved giving her the longitude and latitude coordinates and then being asked to describe what she saw there in her mind.

She was brought to crime scenes, and through a process called derma-optic perception, was asked to touch and feel objects that victims of a crime may have handled. Usually she was able to provide the fragments of a clue. Garcia also worked for an organization called Parents of Murdered Children for many years and while her assistance sometimes led to big breaks, Garcia is careful not to assume full credit.

Deferential and humble, Garcia calls herself "just a tool...I never solved any case. The investigators solved them."

Today, Garcia has found peace of mind at last. "I've become OK with my ability," she says. "I have my own spirituality that I don't push on anyone else." She still works occasionally, but avoids criminology. The dark id of the human psyche had proven too much to bear. Instead, her interests now reside in the paranormal. Asked why, and Garcia says earnestly, "It's fun, it's lighter." This is certainly true of her rewarding experience with the Pink Lady of Yorba Cemetery.

Garcia had first heard of the Pink Lady when she came across an article about the legend in 1982. According to a follow-up article in the *Fullerton Tribune* by Carol Cling, Garcia initially treated the article with skepticism.

"This is bogus, we've been there," Garcia says when asked about her initial impressions. "I just thought it was a bunch of hype." Given the skepticism with which many might view her abilities, it's ironic that Garcia initially found the story of the Pink Lady questionable. Of course, that skepticism withered.

"I've got a completely open mind since then," she says, laughing at her doubts.

Garcia went to Yorba Cemetery on June 15, 1982, where she joined an expectant crowd eagerly awaiting the Pink Lady's arrival. With her skepticism in tow, Garcia watched and waited. What followed next defied all of her expectations.

Garcia looked around the cemetery and then, something drew her attention to the rear of the cemetery. As she "tuned into" the gravestones, Garcia sat down upon the grass and began "to sift through the thought forms, wishes and hopes of the spectators, into the realm of infinite spirit." Her gaze had settled upon an area near the grave of a Castillo, a member of one of the earliest pioneer families to settle the area. Within her mind's eye, Garcia saw the figure of a woman.

She told Cling that she could sense the presence of "a frail, young-looking woman with sandy blonde hair, hazel eyes and a cream-colored dress," a far cry from the pink gown that most had seen her wearing before. The image walked through the cemetery and Garcia followed it before she faded from view. With the spirit now gone, Garcia was left curious and frustrated with unanswered questions. And so began Garcia's investigation of the Pink Lady, a campaign to separate fact from fiction, to diffuse the myths and legends about the Pink Lady. Before Garcia was finished, she would uncover unexpected information regarding one of Yorba Linda's most famous residents.

The legend of the Pink Lady begins at the dawn of the last century (although Garcia's research has determined that accounts of the Pink Lady did not begin appearing until the late 1970s). The year was 1910 and it was spring, a hopeful time for a young girl whose prom night was quickly approaching.

The young girl was the slender, attractive daughter of the prominent Yorba family. She was intelligent and charming, causing many of Yorba Linda's bachelors to clamor for her attention, but unfortunately for them, she believed that she had already found her one true love. She was young and still innocent enough to believe in a love that nothing could ever taint or destroy. All that would change on one fateful prom night.

That night, her boyfriend arrived at her ranch house in a horse-drawn carriage. She greeted him at the door, a vision of beauty in her pink gown. He looked quite resplendent in his evening finery and she had convinced herself that she loved him and that his love was as deep and true. Of course, he had done nothing to convince her otherwise. Which is why it must have come as quite a shock to her when, as the carriage made its way across Orangethorpe Street, her boyfriend leaned over and shoved her from the carriage. She landed awkwardly on the train tracks that ran alongside the street and watched in confusion as the carriage sped away. Before she could lift herself up from the ground, and even before she was able to comprehend fully what had happened, she was crushed by an oncoming train. The girl was buried in Yorba Cemetery, and would forever be known as the Pink Lady. No one seems to know what happened to her beau.

This account has been told and retold over the years with slight variations. There are many people who will argue that the Pink Lady wasn't pushed from the carriage but fell, and that she did die, but not because a train ran over her. Some claim that the Pink Lady died in an automobile accident along Kellog Drive and not Orangethorpe Street. The core of the stories remain the same: the Pink Lady died far before her time (accidentally or otherwise) and has spent the better part of a century roaming near the grave of Alejandro N. Castillo. However, many details about the Pink Lady have proven elusive. Barbara Garcia may be the woman to shed some light on the mystery.

Garcia sketched out three drawings, each having something to do with the Pink Lady. They depict a woman who appeared in Garcia's mind, as well as a church, an automobile burning in flames and a book. They're all pieces of a puzzle; unfortunately, no one knows what the final picture is meant to look like. Further intrigued, Garcia turned to another of her skills to provide illumination. Using a process called automatic writing, Garcia believed that she was able to communicate the thoughts and desires of the Pink Lady's spirit.

"Psychic writing," Garcia says, "is a strange thing. Sometimes, I'll write and it just looks like a bunch of scribblings. The words are sometimes connected, sometimes not. You've got to work to dissect that page...the most bizarre thing is some of it looks like a foreign language to me...I've never even translated some of them." Luckily, the Pink Lady chose to communicate in English.

When sketching or writing, Garcia, according to Cling, says that "I'm not aware of what's going on...[my pencil is controlled] by a spirit, an energy, an intelligence." It's as if the Pink Lady had entered her very mind and discovered a vessel through which she could speak and be heard. And speak she did. When Garcia read what words she wrote after the session, she was a little surprised to discover that the Pink Lady, despite the stories, had little, if anything, to do at all with the Yorbas.

"My family not here, just one. I look for my family, my home: where are they, not here. I am a free spirit, let me go in peace and peace be with you." These were the words that Garcia had transcribed. Other statements she had written down only served to deepen the intrigue: "I was well, but then I had an illness, part of my death." When Garcia focussed on a name, she wrote "Ellie." When she asked about the gravesite that she reportedly appeared beside, she wrote, "No that grave is not mine, I have no stone but I am buried beside that grave."

If these statements were indeed those of the Pink Lady, then the common belief that she is descended from the Yorba family may be completely false. Either that, or her spirit has proven remarkably incapable of searching the tombstones of Yorba Cemetery. Don Bernardo Yorba's headstone, after all, is rather hard to miss, as it is a hulking piece of marble that dominates the small cemetery. The Pink Lady, Garcia concluded, may not even have been a local girl as most had believed. Garcia received the impression that the Pink Lady had died in the early 1930s from an illness. If the Pink Lady was a student at Valencia High School, then the earliest the Pink Lady could have attended a prom was in 1934, when Valencia graduated its first senior class. This was also a time when very few people were still riding in carriages. Elements of the Pink Lady legend seemed to be withering under close scrutiny and all Garcia seemed certain of was that the Pink Lady was a lost soul. Garcia meant to help her find a way home and all she had were her clues: the drawings, the writing and a name, Ellie, which kept running through her mind.

"Ellie's presence—it overpowered me," Garcia told Cling. "It wanted me to walk. I submitted and was led to the gravesite of Angie C. Bleecker, who died in 1934." From there, Garcia followed a trail that led to Benny Castillo and to Bleecker's son, Earlan Bleecker.

Benny Castillo turned out to be Bleecker's nephew and though he did not immediately recall anyone named Ellie, he soon remembered that a woman named Eloedia De Los Reyes was buried beside his father, Alejandre N. Castillo. Garcia sensed an opening. She returned to Yorba Cemetery and made her way directly to a tombstone at the cemetery's rear. It was the same tombstone beside which she had crouched just days earlier when she had first intuited Ellie's presence. Garcia was ecstatic when she looked down at the tombstone and discovered that it bore the name of Alejandre N. Castillo. At her feet was a bouquet of flowers that Garcia had placed earlier to mark Ellie's grave. Garcia felt confident that she had found Ellie, better known to Yorba Linda as the Pink Lady. The absence of a grave marker didn't deter Garcia. Through her research, she had discovered that "in many cases, the lack of funds [for many families] had resulted in surreptitious interments under the cover of darkness without any marker or identification." It wasn't uncommon to bury the recently deceased atop the long dead. The picture was still hazy and fuzzy, but for Garcia it was beginning to come slowly into focus.

Her excitement intensified when she spoke with Earlan Bleecker. At his home, Garcia showed him the sketches that she had drawn, hoping that one of them might trigger a memory and help her learn more. Her instincts proved fruitful, as Earlan Bleecker recognized the church that she had sketched in her trance. It was the San Antonio-Yorba Church and he went on to describe how he had played often behind that church, in and around the adobe ruins that squatted there.

When asked if he knew anything about the Castillo family, Earlan Bleecker went on to describe how various members of the Bleeckers had married into the Castillo family, as well as into the Garcia and De Los Reyes families. Most intriguing was that the name Ellie, which had mysteriously come to Garcia's mind, touched something in Earlan Bleecker's memory.

"He recalled an Ellie who he believed had married a Castillo," Garcia told Cling. "But no one knew what had become of her after the couple had broken apart. He described her as an attractive woman, slender and fair in complexion with light brown hair." Garcia, no doubt, must have been elated to hear how closely his memory of Ellie meshed with the portrait she had sketched. Even if Earlan Bleecker couldn't be entirely sure that the woman in Garcia's drawings was a definitive portrait of Ellie, Garcia appeared to be getting close to the Pink Lady's identity. Would Garcia help the Pink Lady find her way home? Garcia believes that she has.

Walking through Yorba Cemetery, Garcia can no longer sense the presence of the Pink Lady and believes that her spirit has, at long last, found some sort of peace and understanding. The psychic is not completely certain who Ellie may have been in life. The information she received was a mad jumble of different names, people and places that, without further cooperation from the families involved (and they are reluctant to give it), even she is unable to decipher. But Garcia still feels confident enough that she has, at the very least, uncovered an account that is closer to the truth than the oft-repeated legend of the Pink Lady. The absolute truth, however, continues to prove elusive. Despite it all, Garcia considers the experience one of the "most exciting investigations" she's ever performed.

Mount Carmel Cemetery

CHICAGO, ILLINOIS

During his short but eventful life, Al Capone was rarely upstaged. The fearsome and notorious mobster, immortalized by both television and film in *The Untouchables*, ran Prohibition-era Chicago's crime syndicate with ruthless efficiency until treasury agent Eliot Ness finally ended his reign. Capone had evaded charges for the sale and manufacture of alcoholic beverages, which were prohibited under the Volstead Act for years. He was finally convicted on charges of tax evasion and was sent to serve his sentence at the U.S. Penitentiary in Atlanta. Yet even in prison, Capone continued to enjoy the benefits of his position through the thousands of dollars that he'd smuggled in the hollow handle of a tennis racket.

That all changed in 1934, when Capone was sent to Alcatraz, the prison island far removed from the splendor and privilege that had come with his criminal empire. As powerful as he had been, Capone could not escape the frailty of his own life. Syphilis, which he had contracted as a young man, was beginning to ravage his mind; by the time he was released in 1939, he bore little resemblance to the cruelly intelligent man he once was. And though he spent the last remaining years of his life amid the splendor of his Palm Island estate, he was rarely coherent and cognizant. He died in 1947 of cardiac arrest. His body was brought back to Chicago where he was laid to rest in the lavish Mount Carmel Cemetery. His tomb still draws tourists from all over the world, testifying to the grim fascination that many still have for Al Capone. But in death, Capone no longer attracts attention as he once did. In Mount Carmel Cemetery, his fame is often dwarfed by another spirit: the incorruptible Julia Buccola Petta. More on her later.

Mount Carmel Cemetery was among the first cemeteries to serve Chicago's west side and was the creation of the Most Reverend Patrick A. Feehan, the first archbishop of Chicago. In 1895, Feehan purchased a plot of land that, at the time, was better known as Buck Farm. It was a scenic estate of rolling hills and woods, spanning 160 acres, though only 32 of those would be used in the creation of Mount Carmel Cemetery. The cemetery was dedicated on August 31, 1900, with the goal of mainly serving the Catholics of the city's western suburbs, though it would later include people from all areas of the city, Catholic or otherwise.

The first lots had been sold months earlier, in May, but the first burial took place on August 4. In 1905, train service to the cemetery was inaugurated. Upon reaching the southwest corner of the cemetery, two men and a bicycle cart transported the casket to the gravesite. But in the early 1920s, the service was discontinued as the age of the automobile dawned.

Removed and relatively insulated from Chicago and its boisterous citizens, Mount Carmel Cemetery prospered along with the other establishments such as the restaurants that ran along Hillside Avenue. In its early days, a trip to Mount Carmel Cemetery was an all-day affair, and many mourners and officials elected to wine and dine in places like Murphy's and Cotugno's before returning to the city. Despite the time and money required for a funeral at Mount Carmel Cemetery, interments continued to rise dramatically.

In 1900, when it opened, the cemetery had only 54 interments in 4 months, the first five of which were children. In 1901, the number grew to 747. In 1902, there were over 1300. A scant five years later, over 3000 were buried in the cemetery. In 1918, with a flu epidemic sweeping the globe, the cemetery set its own single day record for burials with 84; the total for the year was 4619. As recently as 1986, over 1000 people were still being buried each year in Mount Carmel. All told, it is estimated that over 227,000 bodies lie buried beneath the grounds of Mount Carmel Cemetery.

Many of those buried at the cemetery may not be national figures, but to Chicagoans they were cultural, social and religious icons of the city. Within the Priest's Circle, located just inside the Harrison Street Gate, lie the remains of many of Chicago's first priests. At the center of the cemetery is the Bishop's Mausoleum, built between 1903 and 1912, with an interior designed by famed Italian architect Aristide Leonori and decorated with marble quarried from the Catacombs of Rome and Venetian mosaics. Contained within are nine crypts, each holding the bodies of the archbishops and bishops of the Diocese, men who provided solace, comfort and guidance to countless individuals. When Joseph Cardinal Bernardin, the Seventh Archbishop of Chicago, died in 1996 after a much-publicized and lengthy battle with pancreatic cancer, the outpouring of grief testified to the importance of those who lie buried at Mount Carmel. Over 100,000 lined up outside of the Holy Name Cathedral to catch a glimpse of Bernardin as he lay in state. The Bishop's Mausoleum saw over 50,000 visitors pass through the Corinthian columns flanking its entrance in the two months following Bernardin's interment.

A beautiful, lavish site, Mount Carmel Cemetery is a place of contrasts. Though Mount Carmel has long been the favorite resting site for Chicago's priests and bishops, it has also proven popular with the mobsters who represented Chicago's underside in the 1920s. Entombed within are Al Capone, Hymie Weiss, Frank Nitti and Sam Giancana. Capone's notoriety has led to the repeated theft of his relatively simple grave marker. Even at 125 pounds, the grave marker has proven itself a souvenir difficult to resist.

Just 80 feet from the Bishop's Mausoleum is a tall stone obelisk to mark the grave of the infamous Dion O'Banion. In life, O'Banion had been the head of the North Siders, who counted among their number other gangsters such as George "Bugs" Moran and Hymie Weiss. As it was with Capone, O'Banion thrived under Prohibition, running bootlegged liquor to the speakeasies that multiplied like weeds all over the north side. To supplement his supply, O'Banion took to hijacking the booze shipments of John Torrio. Torrio, understandably, wasn't impressed, but when O'Banion offered to sell Torrio his share of the Sieben Brewery for just $500,000, Torrio relented. Or at least he did until he figured out exactly what O'Banion was up to. O'Banion had only disposed of the Sieben Brewery because he knew that federal agents were about to stage a raid on it. He used Torrio as a patsy and took the chance to make some quick and easy money. Federal agents did raid the Sieben Brewery, and Torrio was charged with violating the Volstead Act. Torrio had had enough.

By day, O'Banion operated a legitimate business, a flower shop that thrived on the arrangements and bouquets so popular and customary at gangland funerals. It sat just across the street from the Holy Name Cathedral, where O'Banion had enchanted parishioners with his Irish tenor as a child. Though one might not have suspected it, O'Banion loved working with flowers. He was always in at nine in the morning and never left before closing. In fact, he often worked late hours, snipping and arranging, long after the last customer had left. Ironically enough, Torrio ordered often from O'Banion, so when Frankie Yale, a Torrio associate from New York, came into his shop on November 9, 1924, to place an order for the funeral for Mike Merlo, late Unione Siciliane President, O'Banion suspected nothing. Torrio himself had already placed an order for $10,000 worth of flowers.

The following morning, O'Banion was hard at work in the back of the shop when he heard the tinkling of the bells that hung above the shop's entrance. It was just a little before noon. With his clipping shears still in hand, O'Banion came to the front of the shop where Frankie Yale, flanked by two strangers, greeted him with a handshake. Had O'Banion recognized the two strangers, he might have suspected something. The two men were Juano Scalise and Alberto Anselmi, the favored assassins of Torrio's right-hand man, Al Capone. Unfortunately, the unwary O'Banion accepted Yale's outstretched hand. Yale squeezed O'Banion's hand tightly, refusing to let him go. O'Banion was surprised and tried to pull away, puzzled until he saw Scalise and Anselmi draw their guns. O'Banion was shot five times: twice in the chest, twice in the neck and once in the jaw. Many suspected that it was Yale who delivered the kiss of death, firing one more bullet into O'Banion's lifeless head.

His body lay in state at a funeral home for nearly a week, while thousands filed past his body to catch one last glimpse of the man who had ruled Chicago's North Side. On November 14, his body was driven to Mount Carmel Cemetery and buried in a ceremony that 20,000 people turned out to watch. Cardinal Mundelein, however, refused to allow O'Banion's body to be placed within a consecrated plot; instead, the mobster was buried in an unconsecrated plot that O'Banion had purchased only recently for a friend who had died during a brawl at the Rendezvous Café.

O'Banion's widow, Viola, wasn't pleased with the cardinal's hard-hearted decision. Five months later, she had O'Banion's body moved to the plot near the Bishop's Mausoleum and had a large monument placed over his grave that was inscribed with the words *My Sweet Heart*. For a man who had taken lives ruthlessly in the name of profit, O'Banion was a doting and loving husband, and that was how Viola wanted the world to know and to remember him. Mundelein was furious. O'Banion hadn't even received the last rites and he was now buried in a consecrated plot? The cardinal allowed O'Banion's body to stay where it lay, but Viola's monument was removed.

Many stories are told about those interred at Mount Carmel Cemetery. The accounts, of course, may not be as colorful or as morbidly fascinating as those of Al Capone and Dion O'Banion, but there is one story that manages to be poignant, tragic and illuminating all at once. It is the story of Julia Buccola Petta, who acquired, in death, a measure of fame and celebrity that belied her simple and unassuming existence. To those who know her best, Julia Petta is known simply as "The Bride."

Not much is known about who the Bride really was in life. She has only her name to hint at who she might have been, but it was only in death that she became legend. Petta, from Schaumburg, Illinois, was only 29 years of age when she passed away after giving birth to a stillborn child (though some believed the Bride passed away on her wedding day). Not long after her burial at Mount Carmel Cemetery, Petta's distraught mother began experiencing terrible and haunting visions that came to her in her dreams.

Philomena Buccola tried but couldn't dismiss them as just nightmares brought on by stress or exhaustion. The visions came to her almost every night. She wanted to make peace with her loss, but upon waking she was unable to shake the feeling that her daughter was still alive.

The visions were always the same, but they never diminished in their capacity to shock Buccola. It's not certain what the grieving mother may have seen in her sleep, and perhaps there are some images that just cannot be translated into words. Buccola claimed that her daughter was coming to her, appearing before her and pleading for her body to be dug up. Initially, Buccola had no idea what she should do. Her daughter was dead. Of that Buccola was certain. But how could she explain the frequency and vividness with which her daughter appeared? Buccola was at a loss. An exhumation seemed too extreme. Sometimes the past is better left buried.

But as the years passed, and the visions continued unabated, Buccola became more comfortable with the idea of an exhumation. She had decided that it was indeed her daughter speaking to her from beyond, and if her dead daughter wished it, who was she to stand in the way? She began asking authorities for permission to have her daughter's body exhumed, but her requests went unanswered. Buccola continued to prod the authorities, wearing away their refusals until, six years later, her request was granted.

The coffin was exhumed and everything seemed ordinary. But when the casket was opened, no one could have possibly been prepared for what lay within. To everyone's shock and surprise, Julia Petta's body exhibited no signs of decay whatsoever. Her skin was as clear and rosy as it had been in life. Her hair was still full and thick. Her body wasn't bloated; the skin wasn't desiccated. Absent too was the smell of decay; in its place was a sweet, almost perfumed, scent. If she were lying on a bed and not within a grimy, rotting casket, one would have been completely forgiven for believing that the girl was just sleeping quietly. Petta may not have been alive, but, still, there was something otherworldly at work.

When a body does not decay, that body is considered, like the body of Christ, incorruptible. To some Christians, the corporeal world is a corrupt world, still bearing the taint of original sin. Anything that can decay, such as material possessions and the body's flesh, has been corrupted. It is the eternal and the immutable that are pure. But every now and then, in a rare twist of fate, mere mortals are blessed with bodies that are incorruptible. Many of them are the bodies of saints. The Catholic Church reveres these bodies, treating them as religious relics. While there are doubters who point to inadvertent embalming as the reason behind the incorruptible flesh, the Catholic Church balks at such assertions. Less than one percent of the incorruptible saints, it claims, are the products of extensive embalming. The rest are nothing but unequivocal signs of holiness, proof of the grace and the everlasting goodness of God.

Given the religious significance of an incorruptible body, it is of little surprise to hear that Julia Petta's body was treated with gravity and deep respect following the exhumation. Shortly before the coffin was reburied, a photograph of Petta resting in her casket was taken and put on display on the front of her tombstone. Etched around the photo were the words, "*Philomena Julia Buccola, aged 29. Questa fotographia presa dopo 6 anni morti.*" The Italian means, "This photograph was taken six years after her death." As a further tribute, a life-sized statue of the young bride, wearing her windswept wedding dress and holding a bouquet of flowers, was sculpted and placed atop a monument that marks Petta's resting place. Her grave has become a beacon of sorts to those who might find themselves questioning their faith and their beliefs. And should the monument not provide adequate inspiration, then there is always the specter of

Julia Petta herself. Not surprisingly, Petta's spirit is believed to walk the grounds of Mount Carmel Cemetery.

Her ghost has been seen on many occasions, particularly by teenagers, who sneak into the cemetery as part of a rite of passage. It was, and may still be, a common practice among the students of Proviso West High School. There was even a time when school dances would come to a grinding halt as students, en masse, would tromp down to the cemetery gates and peer through them into the darkness. Though many have come away from Mount Carmel somewhat disappointed, others have been far more fortunate.

It was a dreary day in 1976, with the sort of rain that falls in a slow and steady drizzle that threatens to persist for days. The streets glistened and as cars sped through the puddles, they sent up a cascade of murky brown water. Into one of these cars was crammed a huddled mass of students, returning to Proviso West after a quick trip off the school grounds. When they reached Mount Carmel Cemetery, the driver slowed the car; he had noticed something beyond its gates. Normally, seeing a girl walking through the cemetery might not have been cause for concern. What was she doing? The rain was falling and it was falling hard. The driver turned to his friends and pointed out towards Mount Carmel.

"Hey," he might have said, "you think something's wrong with her?"

Someone piped up from rear seat. "Hey, maybe it's that ghost we're always hearing about. You know—the one whose body never decayed?"

There were nods of recognition all around, though there were some who doubted the ghost's existence.

"Come on," the detractors said, "we're going to be late. It's just someone pulling a prank. It's Halloween for crying out loud. There's no ghost out there. It's just a girl getting wet in the rain."

For a moment, the explanation seemed sound. Halloween was just days away, and if there was ever a time to pull a prank, Halloween was it. But the explanation gave way before the stark reality of it all.

As the car neared the cemetery gates, the woman, clad in a white dress and picking her way through the tombstones, was only a few feet away. The students in the car could see her face, her hair and the details on her dress all so clearly now. And an audible gasp filled the car and then there was silence, save for the anxious and frantic tempo of the falling rain that now seemed to mirror their own heartbeats. The doubters were wrong. The woman in white walking through the cemetery was undeniably and unmistakably the ghost of Julia Petta. Of that fact the students were convinced. After all, they'd never seen someone walk through the pouring rain and remain completely dry.

As hard as it was raining, the woman in white kept walking, oblivious to the elements. The rain passed right through her, like she wasn't even there. Her hair remained perfectly coifed, her dress as closely pressed as it had been on the day of her wedding. It took the honking of multiple car horns before the driver of the car finally remembered that he was driving a car and that he couldn't just stop in the middle of a busy road. He pulled away, but not before stealing one last glimpse of Julia Petta as she continued to wander through the cemetery. She then disappeared from sight.

For one Chicago family, if it hadn't been for the Bride's intervention, they might very well have lost their son for good. A family had left Mount Carmel Cemetery after attending a funeral there. And, for whatever reason (one supposes that these things just happen from time to time through nobody's fault), the family had left their young son behind. They only realized his absence after they had left the cemetery and were already on their way back to their home in Chicago. In a panic, the family turned the car around and sped back to the cemetery as quickly as they could. Not only had they forgotten their son, but they had forgotten him at a cemetery. Who knows what sort of an effect that might have on his healthy, yet delicate, psyche? The parents ran into the cemetery, calling out their son's name. When they heard no response, they began to fear that their child might have wandered off the cemetery grounds. Their imaginations raced. Had he been abducted? Was he lost in Hillside? Was he hurt? Was he alive? They didn't know. All they could do was ask each other what they should do. Fear creased their brows and they prayed that their boy would be found safe and alive.

In what must have seemed like a miracle, the parents' fear gave way to complete relief. They saw a woman in white emerging from the cemetery, clasping their son's hand in hers. He was calm, unruffled, as if he had just gone to a friend's house and was now being delivered home by another parent. The parents ran to their child and swept him up into their arms. Then they turned to the woman in white, only to find themselves alone. The woman in white had vanished. They looked around, eager to thank her for what she had done. Their gazes fell upon the statue of Julia Petta and immediately they recognized her as the woman who had brought back their son. The parents knew well the story behind Julia Petta, about her incorruptible body and its religious significance. Their prayers had been answered.

Rescuing lost children isn't the only way that the ghost of the bride asserts her presence. There are plenty of individuals who may not have seen her ghost, but still profess to have had an encounter with her spirit. According to the Mystical Universe website (www.mysticaluniverse.com), a woman named Ruth Bukowski had an intriguing encounter with the Bride in 1982. Bukowski visited the cemetery on a November day. The air was cool. The cemetery looked very much like a different place—it was almost eerie. But, as Bukowski discovered, summer wasn't through just yet.

As Bukowski walked through the cemetery, there was something unusual in the air. It smelled sweet and fragrant. A floral designer, Bukowski recognized easily the scent.

"I was there in November of 1982," she said once. "The flowers I smelled were definitely baby roses, better known as tea roses." Most perplexing was that roses had already budded, bloomed and withered by November. And while Bukowski originally assumed that the scent might be from bouquets that mourners might have left behind, a quick look around her revealed nothing but bare tombstones, most of them unadorned; those that were bore no tea roses. Bukowski, well versed in Mount Carmel lore, attributed the aroma to none other than the bride of Mount Carmel. It seemed an appropriate choice; there were still those who could recall that a sweet scent had accompanied the opening of Petta's coffin. No one can be certain that it was truly Petta's spirit that was responsible for Bukowski's experience, but it seems that almost anything is possible in Mount Carmel Cemetery.

Indeed, in a place where the saintly and the devilish lie side by side, it's a little comforting to know that Julia Buccola Petta stands, along with the former bishops and archbishops of Chicago, as a symbol of all that can and should be good within the soul.

Silver Cliff Cemetery

SILVER CLIFF, COLORADO

Over a century old, Silver Cliff Cemetery, situated along Mill Street just south of Silver Cliff, Colorado, was first founded in 1878. The cemetery is set amidst the rustic Colorado plains and the snowcapped Wet Mountains. Plots are pristine and clean; some are marked off with simple wrought-iron or wooden fences. Tombstones made of marble, iron and wood mark the dead.

The oldest tombstone among the 600 graves dates from 1880. The cemetery is still open and is still popular with the people of Silver Cliff. Like the cemetery that shares its name, the town of Silver Cliff is a simple, unassuming place with a population devoted to community and rural life.

Once one of Colorado's largest boomtowns, Silver Cliff sprung up from the Colorado plain almost overnight, as prospectors and speculators flooded the area with the hopes of discovering the mass veins of silver rumored exist just below the surface. Miners began digging a shaft into the Geyser Mine in the side of a cliff in 1877, hoping to strike it rich. When the boom busted 23 years later, Silver Cliff, which boasted a population of 5000 at its peak, struggled for its survival.

Silver Cliff has persisted and has become a sort of living museum for the late 19th century. Buildings there have changed little from the time they were first erected. Visitors stopping for a bite or a rest from their exploration of the Frontier Pathway Scenic and Historic Byway, the San Isabel National Forest or the Wet Mountains, all of which are nearby, must surely find stepping into Silver Cliff an unexpected and welcome surprise. In this way, Silver Cliff continues to exist, even if its prosperity does not even come close to rivaling that of its boom days. Today, its population hovers at around 400 people. There are many stories to tell about Silver Cliff, but one alone has drawn visitors and tourists from all over the country and even the world. Silver Cliff Cemetery, after all, is home to some intriguing and mysterious spook lights.

First seen in 1882, the spook lights of Silver Cliff Cemetery have confounded scientists and paranormal researchers, who continue to seek out a plausible explanation for their existence. They are another example in the long list of what paranormal researchers have dubbed Anomalous Luminous Phenomena, or ALP. But unlike other examples of ALP, such as St. Elmo's Fire, the spook lights of Silver Cliff Cemetery have no ready, scientific and provable basis.

According to an article that first ran in the October 27, 1996, edition of the *San Jose Mercury News*, the Silver Cliff ALP are "round and whitish…they usually appear three or four at a time, are silver-dollar size and float among the headstones of the cemetery." Everyone in Silver Cliff, according to Jim Little, then the editor and publisher of the *Wet Mountain Tribune*, had seen the lights at one point or another. Asked what the lights might be, Little said, "It's just one of those quirky things, a phenomenon that's never been explained. One of life's mysteries."

Silver Cliff Cemetery in Colorado

Others have described the lights as blue-white in color; almost all agree that the lights prove elusive when approached. For unknown reasons, the lights inexplicably disappear when people try to get a closer look at them. These orbs are particularly small when compared with others, which usually vary from a half-foot to two feet in diameter. Still, they have proven no less fascinating.

Also referred to as earth lights or ghost lights, the lights appear to be tied to a specific location, leading some people to conclude that they are a geographically based phenomenon. The blue orbs at Silver Cliff are often seen dancing above the headstones, leading some to theorize that they're phosphorous vapors seeping out from crumbling tombstones. Others suspect that they may be balls of methane gas, but detractors of this theory point out that methane burns a bright orange and yellow, not the bluish white of the Silver Cliff lights. Observers have noticed that the orbs tend to appear on days and nights when the sky is overcast and the air is still, leading to the theory that perhaps the lights are little more than town lights reflected off of the clouds.

The lights provoked so much curiosity and interest that in 1969, when *National Geographic* sent a writer to the Rocky Mountains, he made sure to stop at Silver Cliff. Writing about it in that year's August issue, the writer explained that he'd gone to Silver Cliff because "a fellow camper from Kansas had told [him,] 'Drive out to the old cemetery. You'll see something mighty strange.' " The writer wound up exploring the cemetery in the pitch black of an overcast prairie night with Bill Kleine, who, at the time, ran the local campground. The writer described his experience:

> "Do you believe it?" I asked him. "About the lights in the graveyard?"
> "I've seen them plenty of times. This is a good night for them—overcast, no moon."

We climbed out beside the old burying ground and for long minutes, I strained to see something, anything.

"There." Bill's voice was quiet, almost a whisper.

"And over there!"

I saw them…dim round spots of blue white light glowed ethereally among the graves. I found another and stepped forward for a better look. They vanished.

The pair continued to explore the cemetery as Kleine offered different explanations for the lights' existence. He said it might have something to do with phosphorescence "from decaying wood in the crosses or something." Then he offered the idea that it might have something to do with the town lights of both Silver Cliff and Westcliffe, Silver Cliff's sister city.

The *National Geographic* reporter was skeptical about this theory. Silver Cliff Cemetery, after all, was about a mile south of the town itself and even Kleine allowed that there were holes. In fact, he told the writer that he and his wife had seen the Silver Cliff spook lights on nights "when the fog was so thick you couldn't see the towns at all." With no natural, provable explanation for the lights, many researchers have come to the same conclusion that the lights of Silver Cliff Cemetery are supernatural in origin.

Lest one assume that the years have dimmed the spook lights' mystery and allure, the number of paranormal investigations conducted at the site during recent years should dispel the assumption. The Silver Cliff Cemetery continues to attract the curious.

In 2000, two paranormal enthusiasts visited the cemetery. They had long ago heard of the strange lights that appeared and danced above the tombstones. With their curiosity piqued, they decided that they had better take a look at the lights for themselves. Their night did not get off to a good start.

After a long drive down Highway 96 and a short stop in Silver Cliff itself, they pulled onto Mill Street and began driving the mile or so towards Silver Cliff Cemetery. The night was dark and overcast, which they had been told are the perfect conditions for the spook lights to appear.

They arrived with cameras loaded with an assortment of different films. Perhaps they could catch something on their infrared black and white film. With the beams of their flashlights illuminating just the ground immediately in front of them, they picked their way across the cattle guard and planted themselves in the cemetery and waited. And they waited some more. There was something odd about the way the whole place felt. It didn't feel right and began to sap their energy.

Discouraged, they were ready to give up when one of the enthusiasts looked up at the sign over the gate. Feeling somewhat sheepish, but also relieved, the pair realized that they had come to the wrong cemetery. Silver Cliff Cemetery, after all, is not the only one close to Silver Cliff. Just down the road is Assumption Cemetery, a burial ground for Silver Cliff's Catholics. It was this latter burial ground that they had happened upon. Somewhat red-faced, the two enthusiasts returned to their car and drove

The cemetery's so-called spook lights defy explanation.

back the way they came, coming to a stop at another cemetery. This time, they were positive that they'd come to the right place. A fallen wooden sign, written on in white paint, read, in part, "famous for ghost lights reported in *National Geographic*."

The pair gathered their equipment and began exploring the cemetery. They were somewhat disappointed to see that so many of the wooden markers they had read about seemed to have eroded or replaced. The pair began taking photographs and exploring the site, in the hopes of seeing the spectacular.

With their resolve almost spent, the enthusiasts had almost accepted that they would see nothing at all. But then, in the darkness off to their right, they saw the balls. It was exactly as they had read. The lights danced about the graves, flitting one way and then another. They appeared almost whimsical, and for what seemed an eternity, the pair could only stand and watch. But as soon as they began to approach the graves to get a closer look, the lights disappeared. They were slightly disappointed, but had figured that would happen. It always did. They left the cemetery shortly after, realizing only later that they had forgotten to photograph the balls of light. Still, they felt confident in claiming that the lights were proof of the cemetery's haunting. They could not offer any suggestion as to who might be haunting Silver Cliff Cemetery, but pointed out that given its rugged and wild nature during the earliest of its boom days, Silver Cliff must surely have had its share of tragic and grim deaths. Those, of course, could have lead to ghosts occupying the cemetery. In the end, their trip only proved what many had known all along. They did, however, have far more success than the researchers of Xobic Paranormal Investigations (www.xobic.com).

Founded by Douglas and Christine Welty in 2002 and focusing on the paranormal sites of northern Colorado and beyond, Xobic investigated Silver Cliff Cemetery in August 2003. They visited the site twice, once during the day and once at night, and though they were extremely patient, waiting for two hours beneath a cloudy and moonless sky, they saw nothing.

"We were rather disappointed," they write on their website, "seeing no mysterious lights. Nothing paranormal in the photos either, just some dust orbs." The spook lights may provoke wonder, but they can disappoint too. No doubt Xobic Paranormal Investigations will not consider this first exploration of Silver Cliff Cemetery their last. Such is the magnetism of the spook lights at Silver Cliff Cemetery.

The Salem Witch

SALEM, MASSACHUSETTS

It all started innocuously enough with two girls, Betty Parris and Abigail Williams, in the winter of 1691, in Salem Village, Massachusetts. Reverend Samuel Parris, Betty's father and Abigail's guardian, noticed that the two young ladies weren't quite themselves. They spoke gibberish, communicating in a language only they could understand, and crawled around the floor as if they were animals. More than once, Parris had found the two girls crouched under tables and lying beneath their beds. Puzzled and desperate to help, the reverend tried to find a cure for their afflictions. At last, one doctor felt bold enough to venture a guess. After carefully inspecting the girls, he came to the conclusion that they were possessed by the devil. The diagnosis forever altered the course of Puritanism in the New World.

Salem was founded in 1626 by Roger Conant and his Puritan followers. Prosecuted and vilified in England, the Puritans had arrived in the New World with hopes of establishing a sanctuary in which they could practice their beliefs without fear and condemnation. They wanted to shape the New World with their own religious and political values. But the North American continent was untamed territory, with an indigenous population who viewed the Puritans as encroachers. Native American attacks were commonplace, creating a taut atmosphere that only worsened when the British Governor of

Massachusetts, Sir Edmund Andros, was removed from office in 1689 after the Glorious Revolution in England. Andros' absence created a power vacuum, which provided the opportunity for the residents of Salem Village to finally seek independence from Salem Town.

In 1689, villagers appointed Samuel Parris as their new reverend and leader in their push for their own township. Parris and his supporters believed that Salem Town had become too mercantile, too detached from the strict beliefs of the Bible for the farmers to accept. Opposing Parris were those who had no wish for independence. His appointment polarized residents who had long feuded over everything from land rights to the appointment of reverends. Tensions ran high and villagers began to turn on one another, fearful that the outside world was encroaching into their lives.

At the urging of their elders, Abigail and Betty, along with a group of other children accused of being possessed, began to identify those they believed responsible for the devil's work. On February 28, 1692, arrest warrants were issued for the Parris' native slave girl, Sarah Good and Sarah Osbourne. Charged with witchcraft on March 1, the three women were imprisoned. And so began the infamous Salem witch trials.

Before the year was over, close to 300 individuals were arrested and imprisoned for practicing witchcraft. Jails throughout Massachusetts swelled beyond capacity. Many of those accused were, of course, not witches, and only guilty perhaps of getting into a disagreement with a fellow villager. Denouncing an individual as a witch was fast becoming the preferred method of revenge in Salem

Village. Death was a trial's inevitable conclusion. Of course, by the time most people were tried, they may have seen death as a saving grace.

The Salem Jail, an oak timber building completed in 1684, may have had no bars in its windows, but every attempt was made to make confinement as uncomfortable and inhuman as possible. Prisoners paid for their meals and the salaries of those who had confined them—the magistrate, the sheriff and the hangman. It was an ironic twist that the prisoners were even forced to pay for the fetters, chains and cuffs that kept them shackled. They were given water, but hardly enough to moisten their parched throats. Torture took place so often that it became routine; villagers continued to meet at the jail where they played chess and checkers, while prisoners screamed and pleaded for relief. Many died in the Salem Jail. In a final act of injustice, their family members had to pay for the body's removal. For months, those individuals accused of witchcraft were held in the squalid, over-crowded and rat-infested institution. A trial at least got them out of the jail, but thereupon followed an oxcart ride to Gallows Hill.

Trials didn't begin until June, while the village waited for England to appoint a new governor. At the time, about 80 people had been moldering away in Salem Jail, waiting for a trial. Of all the cases tried, no one was found innocent of practicing witchcraft. Death could only be avoided by pleading guilty and supplying other names. By the end of November, when the madness of Salem Village finally abated, 20 people—7 men and 13 women—were dead. All of them, except one, were hanged atop Gallows Hill.

An artist's depiction of Puritans with an accused witch

Among the victims were a once-respected minister and a constable who had been accused of witchcraft himself after he refused to arrest anymore alleged witches. Most of the victims, not surprisingly, were connected to Native American attacks that had plagued the village for years. Nineteen of the accused had been hanged; only one, 80-year-old Giles Corey, had not been.

A farmer and devout Puritan, Giles Corey was accused of witchcraft in the spring of 1692. Abigail Hobbs had named Corey as a witch when she was confessing to her own involvement in witchcraft. So did Ezekiel Chevers and John Putnam, Jr., who named Corey on behalf of Ann Putnam, Mercy Lewis and Abigail Williams. According to Ann Putnam, a specter bearing more than a passing resemblance to Corey had appeared to her on April 13, and demanded that she write in the devil's book. She also added that the ghost of a murdered man had appeared before her and blamed Corey for his death. Abigail Williams called him a "dreadful wizard" and others claimed that not only had Corey's specter tempted them, but also that it had assaulted them.

Corey was an easy mark. He had arrived in Salem Village in 1659 and acquired a large farm just south of the village. The Porters, one of Salem Village's more influential families, became his close friends, so it was easy for Corey to become a full member of the church. Nevertheless, people saw him as cold and self-interested. Corey's reputation became more suspect when he beat a farm worker to death in 1675. He did little to improve upon the impression when he chose to testify against his wife, who had also been accused of witchcraft, and then recanted his testimony.

Given his association with the Porters, who had a long-standing feud with the Putnams in the community, he was likely a convenient scapegoat for the Putnam family. It was also possible that Corey had openly criticized the witch-hunt. Whatever the reasons, on April 19, 1692, exactly one month after his wife had been arrested, a warrant was issued for Giles Corey.

Corey's hearing began in September. It seemed that the villagers, in their frenzied state, were more concerned with vengeance. The testimony of nearly a dozen witnesses all but guaranteed Corey's conviction. He pleaded not guilty to the charges, but Corey chose to stand mute when he was asked to appear before "God and his country." This was Corey's final act of defiance. He knew all too well that a trial before a jury was a sham and that a conviction would lead a public hanging. His punishment for refusing a trial by jury was the sentence of *peine forte et dure*, a gruesome and cruel punishment that had been outlawed by the government of Massachusetts.

In the middle of September 1692, Corey was led away from the Salem jail and taken to a field where a crowd of villagers had gathered to watch him die. His clothes were removed and then he was asked to lie down upon the grass. A board was placed upon his chest; atop of the board, heavy rocks and stones were placed. Increasing weight was pressed upon him until either his spirit or his body broke. For three agonizing days, Corey lay beneath the stones. Corey made his last words memorable ones. To the surprise and grudging admiration of those gathered,

Giles Corey was the only person ever to be executed by "pressing." Many accused witches were hanged.

Corey managed to whisper, "More weight." Nothing could break his refusal to stand trial. He chose to embrace death. Corey's body was buried in an unmarked grave atop Gallows Hill, the same site where his wife was hanged on September 21, 1692. He remains the only man to have been pressed to death in the United States.

Authorities may have viewed Corey's particularly gruesome death as a deterrent, but if some historians are to be believed, it may have had the exact opposite effect. News of Corey's death spread quickly through New England and the public was aghast. Some credit Corey's defiance with helping to publicize the gross injustice of the Salem witch trials and to build public opposition. Even in death, Corey was not silenced.

As its people suffered, so too did Salem Village. Fearing that they might be accused next of witchcraft, people gathered their belongings and fled with their families to New York. Their crops, left untended, rotted away. Their herds of cattle went unfed. Sawmills came to a stop as workers were arrested for witchcraft, while others could often be found at the local jail or atop Gallows Hill, gawking and watching. Headed for a crisis, Sir William Phipps, the new Massachusetts governor, demanded an end to the witch trials in October.

Spurred by the year's atrocities, including Corey's pressing death, Boston-area clergy led by Increase Mather published an appeal: "Cases of Conscience Concerning Evil Spirits." Worried that the innocent were being condemned to death, Mather denounced the trials, questioning both testimony and evidence. He wrote, "It were better that ten suspected witches should escape than that the innocent person should be condemned." Though the trials did end when Governor Phipps refused to allow "spectral evidence" to be admitted, individuals already arrested weren't all released until the following spring.

Today, a tour through Salem is like a trip back in time, since many of its homes and buildings are protected and preserved as National Historic Sites. Gallows Hill still looms over the city. At 310 Essex Street, there's the Witch

House, a building that has remained relatively the same since the 17th century. The house was owned once by Judge Jonathan Corwin, one of the Salem witch trials' chief magistrates. His home is the only structure still standing from those dark, turbulent of days in Salem history. The legacy of the Salem witch trials exerts a tremendous influence upon the city and is writ large in the memorials, museums and sites dedicated to those proceedings. Today, Giles Corey's presence can still be felt in the Howard Street Cemetery. It is there that the Salem witch trials' most infamous victim still calls out in defiance.

Howard Street Cemetery opened in 1801, just next to Salem's old jail, which used to house those accused of witchcraft. Indeed, although the exact location of Corey's pressing death is uncertain, it is likely that he perished somewhere within the grounds, which would later become Howard Street Cemetery.

If it is Corey's spirit that lurks among the tombstones of the cemetery, then he could not have a more tranquil and bucolic home. The land is uncluttered, just a broad field of grass bordered by fences and towering trees. Among those entombed at Howard Street are relatives of Nathaniel Hawthorne as well as other luminaries of the 19th century.

Rumor has it that when Corey died, the board beneath which he had lain was broken into pieces and its planks used in the fences of homes and other buildings in the area. People still tell stories of how those planks would resist the erosion, remaining and unblemished even years after they were first erected. Homes that sat behind these

Early 20th-century photograph of Gallows Hill

particular fences were said to be notoriously haunted; homeowners were disturbed by loud noises and strange, bright lights into the night—the result of a curse Corey called down before his death. It's not known if there's any truth to those accounts, but they do testify to Corey's powerful grip upon the imaginations of Salem citizens, who more than likely felt guilt for that particular chapter of their past.

The Old Jail, restored and open to the public, and has been recreated faithfully. It's a grim place just that reminds visitors of the havoc wrought upon human souls imprisoned there. It's said that on nights that are still and when the moon is full, Corey howls once again in agony. His screams have frightened more than one passerby.

His is a mournful spirit, one whose grim and melancholy disposition permeates the very air through which he walks. People who have seen Corey's spirit have reported feeling overwhelmed by his sadness, often needing to sit down to collect themselves. Others, who carry on watching, find themselves rubbing their arms and huddling against themselves to ward off a sudden and inexplicable chill. It doesn't work, of course, for it's the sort of chill that abates only after Corey's spirit has faded into the darkness of night.

Corey's continued presence at Howard Street Cemetery is a potent reminder of the suffering too many experienced during the year 1692. While Salem has evolved into a quaint and quiet Massachusetts town, it will always be known for its witch trials. Corey's spirit ensures that people will not soon forget the mass hysteria that robbed individuals of their rights and their lives.

Oakland Cemetery

ATLANTA, GEORGIA

While a cemetery may be a home for the dead, at the same time it is a place where the past has taken root and flourished. If one should stop, one might hear the shout of genius, the lament of tragic youth or the sigh of the lonely dreamer. The bodies may be decaying, but still they speak, sometimes literally, asking that the past be not forgotten. In Atlanta, past and present converge in the Oakland Cemetery; here, you'll find interred citizens from all walks of life who contributed to Atlanta's history.

In 1821, yeoman farmers were beginning to arrive for the land lotteries. More people arrived when the site became the terminus of the Georgia Railroad and the Western and Atlantic Railroad, creating a rough and tumble area of rail hands and prostitutes by 1837. Ten years later, the town of 10,000 voted to change its name from Marthasville to Atlanta. Young people were drawn to the town and its thriving economy. But as the population grew, so too did the need for public burial grounds. Within three years, the self-proclaimed founding fathers of a newly civilized Atlanta purchased six acres on the east part of town for use as a cemetery. The first man to be interred was a Chicago doctor who passed away in 1850 while in Atlanta for a convention. Terrified as he was of being buried alive, Dr. James Nissen had asked for his throat to be slit before he was lowered into the ground.

After 17 years, the cemetery spanned 88 acres. In 1872, what had been City Cemetery became Oakland Cemetery, so named in honor of the numerous oak trees on the property. By the late 19th century, the final plots of Oakland Cemetery were sold. Buried within the original six acres of land are the early influential citizens of Atlanta, including six state governors, 24 mayors, senators and other officials. Dr. Joe Jacobs is buried here; he owned a pharmacy where an entrepreneur created a concoction he called Coca-Cola. Bob Jones, winner of the Grand Slam of golf in the 1920s, lies in the same ground as Margaret Mitchell, author of *Gone with the Wind*. Those less famous are buried in Potter's Field, where there are over 17,000 unknown bodies interred under a single monument.

Today, over a century later, little has changed in Oakland Cemetery. Besides the paving and bricking over of the old dirt roads, the cemetery has remained the same. It is considered a Victorian cemetery. To walk through its grounds is to be thrust back to the Victorian age of elaborate headstones, sculptures and mausoleums. But there are other periods of history to see here too.

There is a plot of land called "The Black Section," where black slaves were buried, identified by both their name and their owners', before the Civil War. After the war, blacks continued to be buried here. Just west of the original six acres stands a 65-foot obelisk made of granite from Stone Mountain. When first erected, it was the tallest structure in Atlanta. This monument marks off the Confederate section where bodies of unknown Confederate and Union soldiers are interred within. Notables lying here include Alexander Hamilton and Brigadier General W.S. Stephen.

In July 1864, Atlanta was home to more than 20,000 people. Shortly after, General William Sherman began his march through Georgia. By November, fewer than 1000 residents were still in Atlanta when the city began to burn. Bodies of the dead soldiers were piled in trenches in Oakland Cemetery and then buried during the last hours of the attack on Atlanta. Still others arrived from a makeshift hospital blocks away in Cabbagetown. By the end, over 3000 Confederate and 16 Union soldiers would come to call Oakland Cemetery home.

Watching over dead soldiers is a 30,000-pound marble lion, lying on a base 17 feet high. The war monument is based on a similar sculpture in Lucerne, Switzerland. The lion lies prostrate, its heart pierced by an arrow, its head cradled by the stars and bars of the Confederate flag, honoring those who died for their ideals.

During November or December, it is said that if people listen carefully, they may hear a roll call in the distance and the voices of the dead soldiers answering to their names.

Greenwood Cemetery

DECATUR, ILLINOIS

Even in a state with such celebrated haunted cemeteries as Bachelor's Grove, Resurrection and Mount Carmel, Greenwood Cemetery still stands on its own as one of the most haunted cemeteries of the United States. Located in Decatur, Illinois, it has been the focus of many paranormal investigations, proving so popular with enthusiasts that the cemetery found itself forced to ban investigations of the place that took place after dark. But what could possibly be lurking within Greenwood Cemetery to invoke such fascination?

Greenwood Cemetery may only have been founded in 1857, but it had already been used for centuries as a burial land not just for settlers, but also for Native Americans. No doubt its long and storied past has contributed heavily to its ghostly reputation. Folklore surrounding Greenwood Cemetery ranges from ladies in white to strange, spectral lights to fallen Confederate soldiers. It's a hodgepodge of the paranormal, to be sure.

Like many old cemeteries, Greenwood Cemetery fell prey to vandals. By the 1920s, they had knocked over and defaced tombstones and left debris from graveyard parties. Little wonder then that the cemetery was abandoned and allowed to disintegrate further until finally, in the latter half of the 20th century, civic-minded individuals, determined to save Greenwood Cemetery, banded together to begin to restore it.

In the middle of Greenwood Cemetery stands a weather-beaten, moss-covered and windswept staircase. It begins in a Decatur street crescent and leads up to four aged tombstones, whose faces have almost eroded, leaving just ghostly traces of the Barrackman family. Their family plot provides the backdrop for one of Greenwood Cemetery's more celebrated ghosts: the weeping woman. After all, it is upon the top step of the staircase where the weeping woman is most often seen.

No one seems to know who she might have been in life, not even paranormal enthusiast Troy Taylor, who discussed her during an interview for *Illinois Country Living* in October 1997. Given her fondness for the top step of the staircase, it might seem logical to assume that perhaps the girl is a relative or friend of the Barrackmans.

"She just sits here and cries," Taylor said in the interview, "she never makes a sound." Little of the weeping woman story has changed over the years. She is most often seen in a long, sweeping period dress that would look odd on anyone wearing it in downtown Decatur. Her body is translucent, slightly opaque, which is not surprising considering that ghosts will appear in a vaporous form. Should one wish to catch a glimpse of the weeping woman on the Barrackman staircase, Taylor advises that visitors come at sunset. "She's never been seen during the day and never after dark," he told *Illinois Country Living*. Taylor should know. He is the author of an entire book dedicated to the paranormal phenomena of Greenwood Cemetery and a veteran of countless paranormal investigations undertaken in the United States. Why the ghost cries, however, is still a mystery.

It can't be from loneliness, since she is not the only spirit who inhabits Greenwood. There is another mournful spirit that is often seen wandering aimlessly among the tombstones. She is always seen in her pristine white wedding dress. Her face is inscrutable, betraying little emotion. But judging by her solemn appearance, her life might not have been a happy one. Perhaps her marriage was short-lived? Many witnesses have been tempted to speak with her, but she disappears, fading into the air from which she appeared so mysteriously. Taken together, the bride and the weeping woman provide an interesting counterpoint to the often frightening and bizarre occurrences that are rumored to have taken place inside the now razed mausoleum.

Torn down in 1967, the mausoleum was a place of the macabre. Few people wanted to pass by the building, and would be terrified whenever the spirits of the mausoleum exerted themselves. Like most of the cemetery, the mausoleum had fallen into serious disrepair and it seemed as if the bodies interred within felt that this state of affairs could not be allowed to pass unnoticed. To garner attention, they filled the air with piercing shrieks and cries that were never forgotten once heard. Just in case their screams failed, the spirits also flooded the building with strange, ethereal lights. The mausoleum was torn down and its bodies, according to Troy Taylor, were placed in a mass grave just across the road. However, the spirits may not have been completely placated. Rumor has it that the site of the former mausoleum was full with paranormal energy. Those sensitive to such emanations often report feeling as if the very air is charged with a tingling electrical energy that shakes them to their very core.

It's a feeling similar to the one felt when people walk through the section of Greenwood Cemetery dedicated to the soldiers of the Civil War. According to Taylor, Decatur was a frequent stop for trains ferrying captured Confederate soldiers to prison camps. In one particularly gruesome episode, a train was passing through and stopped near Greenwood Cemetery. Many of the Confederate soldiers aboard were ill, so the stop had to be made. No one knows how the epidemic aboard the train started, but all knew that the yellow fever that was taking so many Confederate lives had spread quickly in the confined spaces of the train. Many had died and the very air was fast becoming noxious. A wagon was brought to transport the dead in a mass unmarked plot on the side of the hill. Many bodies were already rotting away in the heat and humidity. Sadly, in their haste to dispose of the dead, Union officials may not have noticed that some of the men were still alive, albeit too weak and too frail to raise their arms or voices in protest. It is horrific to imagine, but they were buried alive.

These are the soldiers who haunt Greenwood Cemetery today. They have startled many visitors to the cemetery, appearing atop the crests of the hilly terrain. Lost and seeking a way home, the soldiers wander Greenwood Cemetery, far removed from their homes in the South. These mournful specters are angry and displaced. Many individuals walking through the Civil War section of Greenwood Cemetery find it a most uncomfortable

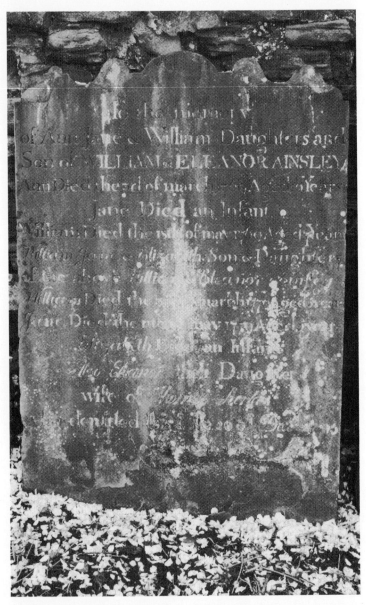

History and tragedy contribute to the hauntings at Greenwood Cemetery in Decatur, Illinois.

experience, often reporting being overwhelmed with a flood of melancholy and unrequited longing.

One day, not that long ago, a man reported an encounter with one of the spectral soldiers. His uniform was frayed and caked with dirt and blood. He moved slowly, as if every step was a Herculean effort. According to Taylor and an account posted on his website (www.prairieghosts.com/greenwd1.html), the soldier turned to the man and asked, "Can you help me? Where am I?" The man stood dumbfounded as a chill passed through his veins. The soldier spoke again. "I just want to go home," he said, his voice heavy with emotion. He then vanished from sight.

Tragedy seems to be common to all the spirits of Greenwood Cemetery, and it's also the underlying cause of the cemetery's mysterious spook lights. Like the lights of Silver Cliff Cemetery, these blue-white orbs appear to have no earthly cause, though their origins are firmly rooted in human suffering.

Years ago, a flood swept through Decatur, claiming hundreds, if not thousands, of lives. When the bodies were recovered, many of them ended up being buried on the southern edge of Greenwood Cemetery. Unfortunately, some of the bodies were and remain anonymous. Their markers are bereft of names. The lights that appear in Greenwood, the orbs that flit among the headstones, are believed to be the spectral remains of those anonymous victims, forever seeking out their burial sites.

There is an assortment of souls within Greenwood Cemetery who have suffered much in life. They are a miserable lot, unlucky in life and, alas, in the afterlife too.

Camp Chase Cemetery
COLUMBUS, OHIO

Do not be fooled by its size. Though it spans less than two acres, Camp Chase Cemetery in Columbus, Ohio, holds national significance for the Civil War and its aftermath. It is hallowed ground, underneath which over 2000 Confederate soldiers lie, far from their homes in Kentucky, Virginia and other Confederate states. These young men left home to defend their way of life and ended up in a prison camp where death was routine.

All those buried at Camp Chase died as prisoners of war. Their suffering passed a legacy of loss and devastation to their survivors. The passing years have not even begun to heal the wounds of the Civil War and people still mourn at Camp Chase.

Named for Secretary of the Treasury and former Ohio governor Salmon P. Chase, Camp Chase opened as a training camp for Union volunteers and as a prison for some political and military prisoners from Kentucky and western Virginia. But with Union victories in 1862 at Fort Donelson, Tennessee, and at Mississippi River Island, more and more Confederate soldiers, and even their black servants, were held at Camp Chase. But life at the prison was far from rigorous for the ranking Confederate officers. They were still able to receive gifts of food and money, and were even allowed to walk the streets of Columbus while imprisoned. When government officials realized what was happening at Camp Chase, they launched an investigation.

It was determined that the men, mostly volunteers, who ran the prison, were ill equipped to handle the running of a military prison and to mete out much-needed discipline. The federal government assumed control of the prison and embittered former Union officers were hired to run the place. They eliminated all the officers' privileges, transferred prisoners to a stockade on Johnson's Island, banned visitors and censored inmates' mail. There was a precipitous decline in living standards at the prison as planners tried to cram more and more Confederate soldiers into the rapidly dwindling space. Men slept two to a bunk in barracks that provided scant protection from the elements. The crowded quarters stood on muddy ground polluted with open latrines and waste. By 1863, over 8000 men were confined at Camp Chase, a prison designed to house less than half of that number. Prisoners strong enough to work were sent to rebuild the barracks and reinforce the fence. The conditions were inhuman.

The close living quarters and lack of proper sanitation had created a breeding ground for diseases from which almost no one was immune. In the winter of 1863, smallpox struck Camp Chase, devastating a population of prisoners who had already been weakened by the cold and their meager diets. In February 1864 alone, close to 500 men contracted the illness and died. The dead were, for a time, laid to rest in Columbus' City Cemetery. Once the Camp Chase Cemetery was established, these bodies were re-interred at the prison.

The buildings of Camp Chase, its prison and barracks, were razed after Lee surrendered his Army of Northern Virginia at Appomattox in 1865. Some of the timber used in their construction was recycled and used as markers for the dead. The stone wall of the cemetery remained, as did the bodies, but little else. Without men or women around to care for the grounds, the headstones were allowed to rot away and what remained was embedded in overgrown weeds.

Union officer William H. Knauss was on his quest to mark the graves of Confederate soldiers who'd perished at Antietam when he discovered this overrun burial site. Knauss, who himself had been left for dead at Fredericksburg, wanted to heal the country and to bring its people together not just in law but in spirit once more. What he saw at Camp Chase shocked him.

Knauss pushed for the cemetery's recognition as a site with both national and historic significance. He viewed the Confederate soldiers as Americans—men whose sacrifices should not be forgotten. They may have once been the enemy, but peace had been secured and they were kin once more. In 1896, the first memorial service was held at Camp Chase. In time, the services would attract men and women in the thousands, and the services continued to take place annually on the Sunday closest to June 3, the birthday of Confederacy President Jefferson Davis.

On June 7, 1902, Ohio Governor George Nash presented and dedicated a granite arch, built with donations from the public. It stands just beyond the cemetery's wrought-iron fence, at its feet lies a misshapen boulder set amid tiny flowers; etched into the stone are these words:

A monument to the Confedate dead interred at Camp Chase
Cemetery in Ohio

"2260 Confederate Soldiers of the War 1861–1865 Buried
in This Enclosure." Perched atop the granite blocks is the
bronze statue of a Confederate soldier who stands in quiet
vigilance with the word "Americans" inscribed at his feet.
In 1906, Congress replaced the worn wooden headboard
with white marble tombstones. It's a powerful monument, one that asks for both unity and forgiveness. The
United Daughters of the Confederacy return to Camp
Chase Cemetery each year, timing their visit with the
annual memorial service, at which time they pay tribute
to the dead and adorn the bare graves with flowers.

But it appears that someone thinks that the United Daughters of the Confederacy doesn't pay enough tribute to both soldier Benjamin Allen of the 50th Tennessee and to a soldier whose name is unknown. These two graves receive the special attention of Camp Chase's resident spirit, the Lady in Gray.

The Lady in Gray acts as the conscience of those who find it easier to forget than to remember. She has visited the cemetery for years and not even her own death has prevented her from doing so. She is still paying her quiet respects, often to the shock and amazement of visitors not expecting to see a ghost.

No one knows who the Lady in Gray might be. Few facts are available to hint at the spirit's identity. All that anybody really knows is that she has a particular fondness for Benjamin Allen and the unknown soldier. She leaves fresh flowers for them, often at night when the cemetery's wrought-iron gates are closed and locked. Ghosthunters come to Camp Chase Cemetery eager to catch a glimpse of the lady at work.

The Shadowseekers is an Ohio-based organization "dedicated to researching and understanding the strange and unusual," driven and guided by the simple question "What will it take to make you believe?" To that end, they have conducted hundreds of investigations ranging through all of Ohio's 88 counties in their quest to legit-imize paranormal research.

On April 13, 2003, the Shadowseekers converged upon Camp Chase Cemetery to uncover the truth about its famous Lady in Gray. For an hour and a half they walked the grounds, taking photographs and interviewing the

During one impromptu investigation, intrepid teens ran across the Lady in Gray among the cemetery's gleaming white headstones.

cemetery's employees and those who worked near it. They saw little evidence of the ghost's presence, as the graves of both Benjamin Allen and the unknown soldier were unadorned, with nary a freshly cut flower in sight. The wind that whistled through the cemetery made it impossible to record any ambient voices or sounds they might have picked up. The people they interviewed all claimed not to have seen anything strange and unusual, but of course they had heard the stories about the Lady in Gray.

Slightly discouraged from their earlier results, the Shadow-seekers found one of their photos revealed what might possibly be the presence of a spirit, but they were unwilling to label it as definitive proof of the Lady in Gray. Champ Chase Cemetery remains an open investigation for the Shadowseekers, who have promised to return to the cemetery for further interviews.

The Lady in Gray has also eluded another paranormal researchers' group, the Ghosts of Ohio. They have journeyed to the cemetery on numerous occasions, hoping to see physical evidence of her existence. But like the Shadowseekers, they have yet to encounter anything strange or unusual. Indeed, in all the times they have explored Camp Chase Cemetery, the Ghosts of Ohio have yet to even see a single freshly cut flower grace Benjamin Allen's grave. One time, they did see flowers adorning the grave of the unknown soldier, but their "initial excitement...quickly faded when we realized the arrangement was plastic...we don't believe the Lady in Gray would stoop to leaving plastic flowers." But while these two paranormal organizations continue to seek out the Lady in Gray, all Frederick Jones (a.k.a. Freddy) has to do to see her is return to his memories.

It hasn't been that long since Freddy Jones was at Camp Chase Cemetery. It's a long journey for him, considering that he rarely leaves his home in Texas where he runs a pizza restaurant in Houston. But despite having left Ohio, he is still a Buckeye at heart and his voice still has a Midwest accent. He returns to Camp Chase every year, determined to follow the example set out by the Lady in

Gray, on the Sunday closest to Jefferson Davis' birthday, to honor those lost in the Civil War.

Freddy had first heard of Camp Chase Cemetery at his elementary school.

"Yeah, it was one of those things," he says. "Kids were always trying to scare each other and one of those stories they always trotted out was about the Lady in Gray at Camp Chase. For me, it was all brand new and of course, it was all exciting," he recalls. Freddy, whose parents had immigrated to the United States from the United Kingdom, hadn't been reared on Columbus' folklore, so when he first heard the stories about the spooks that lurked just in his backyard, he was riveted.

Shy and curious, Freddy walked by Camp Chase too many times to count. Every so often, he would stop and peer through the fence and wonder if what he had heard was really true. But he never could work up the courage to pass through the entrance and always ended up hurrying past the gates, his heart pounding ever so slightly while his hands grew cold and clammy.

When Freddy was 14, he and some other boys were invited to a sleepover at a friend's house. His friend lived in southwest Columbus, just a few streets from Camp Chase Cemetery. As the night progressed, they wanted to do something exciting and daring.

"Someone suggested that we go to Camp Chase," Freddy explains. "We all had our bikes there and just the idea of sneaking out of the house was thrilling." They pedaled across dark streets quickly, ever mindful that the parents might wake up at any moment to check up on them. When they reached Camp Chase Cemetery, they hopped off their bicycles and peered into the gloom that lay beyond the wrought-iron gate. The gate was locked, of course, and the only way to get across was to climb.

"I was pretty reluctant to do that," Freddy recalls. "It's a cemetery for crying out loud, and I'm the fat kid who can't climb fences." But he did it. Following his friends' leads (one of whom had possessed enough foresight to bring along a bathmat filched from the house to lay across the fencetop), Freddy clambered over, pants intact, and found himself standing amid the white marble tombstones of the soldiers he had heard so much about in school.

"It was eerie," he says, "standing there in the dark, and all I could see were these gleaming white tombstones that went on and on in row after row. They looked kind of like teeth, actually."

For a while, Freddy and his friends crept through the cemetery, using a penlight to guide their way. They were seeking out Benjamin Allen's tombstone, to see if the Lady in Gray had set out her freshly cut flowers. But when they got there, they saw nothing but the tombstone illuminated in the glowing circle of their penlight. Disappointed, the boys were also getting sleepy, though no one would have admitted it, and ready to head home.

"Then we heard it," Freddy remembers. "We heard it. And we all stopped and looked at each other. It sounded like there was someone crying inside of that cemetery— these loud, choking sobs."

With straining eyes, they peered and saw the figure of a woman who wore the darkness of the evening like a shroud. Moving with an unhurried purpose through the tombstones, she was carrying a bouquet of flowers that

Camp Chase's small size belies its sizeable historical—and paranormal—legacy.

looked colorless in the evening light. She wore clothing that Freddy had only ever seen in the pages of his history books—the kind of dresses that seemed designed to cover every inch of flesh with their high collars and long pleated skirts. Her face was streaked with glistening tears and she was sobbing.

"It was a little scary, but not nearly as much I thought it might be. It was more awesome than anything I might have expected," Freddy says, his voice measured, even and calm. "She walked, well, it was more like she floated across the ground. She passed right through a couple of trees, but as amazing and incredible as that was, it's her crying, her sobbing, that I haven't been able to forget. That's the stuff that's stuck with me over the years. Sometimes, I can still hear her in my head and whenever I do, I still get goosebumps—up my arms, down my legs, in the small of my back."

Freddy and his friends stared, almost unaware of each other, as the Lady in Gray floated among the tombstones before stopping in front of one. She bowed her head and stood.

"She mumbled something," Freddy recalls, "but none of us could hear what she said. I'm thinking it was probably a prayer or something." When she finished, the Lady in Gray knelt down in the grass and placed the flowers atop the tombstone, then she turned and floated back the way she had came. She passed through all concrete matter, even the wrought-iron fence that surrounds Camp Chase Cemetery, before fading out of view.

Freddy and his friends never forgot that evening at Camp Chase; it formed the basis for friendships that remains strong to this day. They still return every year to Columbus to attend the memorial services.

"Whenever I enter that cemetery," Freddy says, "even when it's a hot and bright sunny day, I still get chills. It's not an eerie thing though. More like the chills you get when you read a really great book or hear a really great song. It still feels as if the Lady in Gray is around. I haven't seen her again, but I'd like to think that she'd be pleased with the way she touched me. I know I am."

Bucksport Cemetery

BUCKSPORT, MAINE

Although Revolutionary War hero Jonathan Buck was so revered and popular that Buckstown was named after him, few people outside of the state of Maine ever utter his name without at least mentioning his allegedly cursed gravesite. His is a legend that has been distorted and exaggerated over time. It is one of revenge, of witchcraft and of a supernatural curse. It's compelling, despite allegations that the story has no basis whatsoever in fact.

Jonathan Buck, born in Woburn, Massachusetts, in 1719, was not a common man. Adventurous, patriotic and dedicated, Buck had a hand in the early shaping of Maine, surveying six plantations in 1762 that would eventually become Bucksport, Orland, Penobscot, Sedgwick, Blue Hill and Surry. At the time, Maine was covered with stands of virgin pine that soared over 100 feet into the sky and stood over 4 feet in diameter. Felling them with nothing but axes and elbow grease was daunting, but without pack animals, clearing them was an even trickier proposition. Hundreds of men worked to clear a fallen tree from the ground, chopping the trunk into manageable chunks that were then fed into a fire. Adding to the settlers' problems was the constant threat of attack from Native Americans as well as an unreliable supply of food and disease. In 1775, the American Revolution threatened Buck and his band of settlers, who had come to Maine to establish their own township. A British naval blockade had isolated them, essentially severing their one and only link to desperately needed supplies. Under siege, men, women and children began dying, forcing the settlers to flee their homes. Buck, 60 years old and suffering from gout, accompanied by his family of six children, walked close to 200 miles to safety in Haverhill. He would not see his home again for another five years.

With the conclusion of the American Revolution in 1783, Buck returned home at last. Nothing was as he had remembered. British troops had burned and pillaged everything they had found there. Buck's spirit, however, was not broken. With renewed determination, he helped rebuild homes and farms. A town was raised, literally, from the ashes. Buck and his family were revered for their dedication and perseverance and, in 1792, what had only been known as Plantation Number 1 was reborn as Buckstown (later changed to Bucksport), in honor of Jonathan Buck. Buck died on March 18, 1795, and was buried in what would become Bucksport Cemetery. His death, while devastating to those who had known and loved him, was inconspicuous enough. No one could have predicted what would happen almost a century later.

In the fall of 1852, seeking to honor their grandfather, Buck's grandchildren had an obelisk, standing 15 feet tall and carved from Blue Hill granite, erected near his grave. It was a fitting tribute to the man who had given so much of himself to ensure the survival of Bucksport. As the years wore on, however, curious locals began to notice something truly strange about the monument. Such are the origins of the Buck monument legend.

It's hard not to notice the strange stain that appears beneath Buck's etched name on the monument and it's not hard to imagine a confused populace, one bred with superstition, seeking to explain its origins with wild and spectacular tales.

The reddish orange stain was innocuous enough at first, but as the years passed the stain only grew and began to resemble, mysteriously, the outline of a woman's leg and foot. Surely, locals whispered, something supernatural and bizarre must be at work. The monument was allegedly replaced twice by Buck's descendants, but each time the leg reappeared and they soon grew weary of replacing it. People were eager to explain the foot's appearance and the resulting theories were so strange and macabre that not even the press could fail to take notice.

According to researcher Valerie Van Winkle, an account of the foot on Buck's headstone first appeared in print in the *Haverhill Gazette* in the spring of 1899. It was this account that became the basis for all other theories concerning Buck's monument.

With its origins firmly and obviously rooted in the hysteria of the Salem witch trials, the *Haverhill Gazette* report transformed Jonathan Buck into a hysterical Puritan, deathly afraid of witches and their sorcery. With his influence, Buck was able to have a woman condemned to death because he believed that she was practicing witchcraft. On the day of her hanging, the woman turned to Buck and proclaimed, "Jonathan Buck, listen to these words, the last my tongue will utter…you will soon die. Over your grave they will erect a stone that all may know where your bones are crumbling into dust…upon that stone the imprint of my feet will appear, and for all time, long after you and your accursed race have perished from the earth, will the people from far and wife know that you murdered a woman." Other accounts are far more lurid.

In one version, Buck and the woman were involved in an illicit affair. Their late night trysts had already led to the birth of one hideously deformed son. Most shocking of all, when the woman was executed she was pregnant again with another of Buck's children. With their deformed son watching, Buck tied her to the door of her home and lit the woman on fire. As the woman writhed and screamed in agony, her leg fell away from her body. The child, unable to bear anymore, ran up, grabbed the smoldering limb, called out a curse and fled into the darkness of the surrounding woods. The leg then appeared upon Buck's monument to mark his crimes. Variations upon this story claim that the boy touched Buck with the charred limb, crippling him for life in an act of divine or hellish retribution.

In yet another account, the mark of the leg was the result not of a witch, but of a cruel and unrepentant murderer. Accused of murdering a woman and amputating one of her legs, the criminal was brought before the Justice of the Peace, who happened to be none other than Jonathan Buck. With overwhelming evidence of the murderer's crime at hand, Buck had no choice but to sentence the murderer to death. But just before the noose was placed around the murderer's neck, he condemned Buck. The result? The foot on the stone.

The leg is plain to see upon Buck's monument and over the years visitors have flocked to Bucksport, eager to

Markings on gravestones can play a large role in cemetery hauntings.

catch their glimpse. To be sure, many of them must have been spurred by the legends surrounding its origins. Some individuals discount even the hint of a witch's curse, proclaiming that Jonathan Buck was nothing less than an honorable and respected man, a town founder and the builder of Bucksport's first saw mill, first grist mill and first boat. Though one might suspect that some of these detractors are motivated to prevent the smearing of Buck's good name, there are historical facts that call into question many aspects of the Buck monument legend.

The basis of the legend rests firmly in the hysteria of the Salem witch trials. While many Puritan communities throughout the northeast did succumb to the mass panic that led to the arrests, imprisonment and executions of hundreds of women and men in 1692, the trials took place a good quarter century before Buck was even born. In fact, there was no record of anyone having been executed by fire in the state of Maine while Buck was Justice of the Peace, according to writers Valerie Van Winkle and Jeff Hutchins. He did not have the power, even if he wanted it, to execute anyone. No accounts of the witch's curse appeared until the story first appeared in the *Haverhill Gazette.*

As for the monument itself, Hutchins is careful to point out, "Stories that the monument had been replaced are untrue. This is the original." But what of the leg? How did the leg appear and reappear despite the best and repeated attempts of people to scrub it away permanently? Stone workers have said that it is not entirely uncommon for strange markings to appear on granite after it has been cut and polished. Metals and minerals within the stone are natural flaws and, over time, oxidize. If the metal is a vein of iron, then oxidation will naturally lead to rust, resulting in the reddish orange color of the stain. Scrubbing only removes the surface and not the iron. Science and fact, it seems, have trumped the legend of Buck's monument.

In the end, it seems likely that there never was a curse laid upon Jonathan Buck, but the story continues to appear. The legend of Buck's monument, with its emphasis upon witchcraft, the supernatural and the fall of an unimpeachable man, is a compelling story that will continue to be told and retold.

Photograph Monument
MURRAY COUNTY, GEORGIA

Jonathan Buck may have a leg and a foot on his tombstone, but one must not forget the strange oddity that was the headstone of one Smith Treadwell. Treadwell may not have had a leg or foot appear on his tombstone, but in a truly eerie twist of fate, an entire face did. The similarities between the two do not end there. As it was with Buck, stories used to explain the face's appearance called into question Treadwell's character, leaving many people angry but no one closer to the truth.

Smith Treadwell, according to Jim Miles in an article that appeared in the June 2003 issue of *FATE* magazine, was a prosperous plantation owner who had risen from obscurity to find success in northern Georgia. He had land holdings in no less than five counties: Murray, Floyd, Bartow, Whitfield and Terrell. Treadwell had arrived in northern Georgia in 1840; shortly after, he married Polly Mobley. His wife died in 1851, but in an odd twist, he married Mobley's sister, Betsy. Though it was common knowledge that his wife had given him permission to do so from her deathbed, Treadwell's hasty marriage to Betsy led some people to question quietly, then loudly, his first wife's passing.

It wasn't long after Treadwell's second marriage that the Civil War erupted across the United States. Georgia, as one of the wealthiest and most prosperous of the slave states, was hotly contested and suffered greatly as Union

General William Tecumseh Sherman slashed and burned his way across the state in the fall of 1864 during his March to the Sea. After the war, many people returned to still smoldering homes. The once-grand plantation homes had been reduced to rubble, fields of cotton and tobacco to ash. Treadwell had wisely avoided the financial ruin that plagued so many in northern Georgia. With the onset of war, he had fled with his family to Terrell County in south Georgia. And while far too gray and wizened for service in the Confederate Army, Treadwell still volunteered and found work as a prison guard at the infamous Andersonville prison camp. He died in 1893 and was buried at his estate in Murray County. A marble monument was erected upon his gravesite.

It didn't take long. Only a year after the marble monument was erected, a strange visage appeared on the marble's face. It was undeniably a face of a man who appeared either perplexed or agitated. A great beard flowed from the chin in sweeping tresses, blending in with the head's hair. Some of those who had been close to Treadwell in life claimed that the image was unmistakably that of their departed friend.

In his article, Jim Miles quoted a former slave, Levi Branham, who had written in his book, *My Life and Travels*, that he "helped bury Mr. Treadwell…within a year, I noticed the picture [on the tombstone]. I think it resembles him very much." A newspaper noted that "the face on the tombstone…is a wonderful likeness of the man…buried beneath it." Some relatives disagreed, but once word of the mysterious face on the tombstone had spread, they were powerless to stop it.

The resulting publicity led to its inclusion in the syndicated *Ripley's Believe It or Not*, bringing this particular phenomenon to national attention. It's not surprising, of course, that Treadwell's Murray County cemetery became the stopping place for tourists. Most of them cared little that the tombstone was, in fact, on private property and came at all hours of the day or night, often interrupting the property owners during meals or sleep to ask their questions. Inevitably, the property owners grew weary of this intrusion into their private lives and could no longer stand answering the same questions.

Perhaps the property owners' recalcitrance led to the disparaging of Treadwell's character. They were unwilling and unable to provide more definitive answers to the face's origins, so people began speculating on their own. As it was with Buck's leg and foot, people whispered that the face was the mark of a cursed man.

Treadwell was a bootlegger, they said. His calm and gentle demeanor was nothing but an act, hiding a secret life in which Treadwell was anything but calm and gentle. He was ruthless, cruel and manipulative. And sure enough, people turned to the strange circumstances surrounding his second marriage. He married his wife's sister, they said in incredulous tones. On her deathbed, his wife gave permission for him to do so, they added with great disbelief. He had to have an ulterior motive, they concluded. Suddenly, in their eyes, it was all too clear. Treadwell, the corrupt and viciously unkind bootlegger, was a murderer too. He had murdered his wife, maybe in collusion with her sister, and then made up the story about her granting her permission. It was a perfect story; after all, his dead wife couldn't speak since he had killed her.

The theories, while most likely nothing more than speculation, only cemented the tombstone's iconic status, garnering more and more publicity. For two decades, visitors swarmed Treadwell's grave. Its popularity, never welcome in the first place, led to the site's vandalism. Tombstones were damaged, stolen and defaced. It was more than Treadwell's descendants could even bear. In 1951, the mania finally ended.

No one knows who the responsible party was, but intrepid thieves made off with Treadwell's gravestone. Miles writes that "it was almost a sense of relief that greeted the theft." Life in Spring Place slowly assumed a semblance of normalcy. When the stone was found, years later, in Mill Creek, the Treadwell family chose not to have it remounted. It rests, instead, in storage, its mysteries and origins safely anonymous.

The End